What will be

A tale of triumph and resilience

Leila Owl

 A Kindle exclusive from KR Publishing, Southampton, UK

© KR Publishing, 2023

The characters and events portrayed in this book are fictitious. Any similarity to real persons, living or dead, is concidental and not intended by the author.

All rights reserved. No part of this publication may be reproduced, or stored in a retrieval system, or transmitted in any form or by any means, electronic, mechanical, photocopying, recording or otherwise without the express written permission of the publisher.

Contents

A Vision	iv
Prologue	v
Chapter 1	1
Chapter 2	5
Chapter 3	7
Chapter 4	13
Chapter 5	16
Chapter 6	20
Chapter 7	27
Chapter 8	33
Chapter 9	38
Chapter 10	49
Chapter 11	57
Chapter 12	64
Chapter 13	74
Chapter 14	80
Chapter 15	86
Chapter 16	92
Chapter 17	96
Chapter 18	108
Chapter 19	116
Chapter 20	125
Chapter 21	140
Chapter 22	146
Chapter 23	153
Chapter 24	159
Chapter 25	166
Chapter 26	172

A Vision

At times I made light of it
And I was free.
Then suddenly I was shown her in a vision
And she was radiant in hue, like a lighted lantern.
Surely she must have been imprinted in my heart
How else could I be so intoxicated by her?
Inside my breast she tick-tocks like a watch
At night when I sleep she comes to sport with me
But at early dawn she leaves
And turns into a rising pillar of dust.
Cilmi Bowdheri Somali Poet c.1910-1941

What Will Be

Prologue

Southampton, United Kingdom 2000

To paraphrase an American cigarette advert, 'she'd come a long way, baby!'

It was autumn, Amina's favourite season. She loved the warm autumnal colours, the way the leaves changed colour and the coolness of the air. She also loved that she got to wear warmer clothes, tweeds, cashmere and boots in her favourite colours, khaki, gold, and tan.

Her husband Dylan hated autumn. 'As soon as the clocks go back, I know we're into winter facing weeks of cold and darkness,' he often told her.

As she came down the stairs this morning, she was wearing an Armani buttermilk leather skirt, an olive-green cashmere jumper, and long, tan Louboutin boots. To top it off, she would throw on her cream cashmere Versace coat. She wondered if she was a tad overdressed; she would only get her hair and nails done at Terry's and then meet her friends for lunch. Earlier this morning, she had taken her daughter Samara to kindergarten and spent an hour in her home gym, followed by another hour languishing in the steam room and sauna adjacent to her temperature-regulated indoor swimming pool. Dylan had already left for his office. At thirty, he was already a millionaire and, along with his investment firm, ran his vast empire of hotels, clubs, and spas from his office in the city centre. She had given herself the day off from her own award-winning advertising agency, confident that no-one would really miss her, the staff might even be pleased that the boss was away for the day.

She walked out of her bedroom, down the palatial stairs and into the vast kitchen. 'Morning, Signora,' the Italian cook greeted her as she sat down alone at the table designed to seat twelve and awaited her breakfast.

Her cup of hot water and lemon juice was already in front of her, and she took small sips from it.

The cook then brought her favourite breakfast, porridge with honey and blueberries, which she ate quickly. Time to get a move on.

'Signora, any preferences for dinner tonight?' He asked.

What Will Be

'No, don't worry, Antonio, we're eating out at the club tonight, see you later', and with that, she was out the door and into the driveway where half a dozen luxury cars were parked. She picked the black Mercedes and drove through the electronic gates, which had swung open onto the main road taking her into the city centre. It wasn't always like this.

Chapter 1

Mogadishu, Somalia, December 1990

The house was large, three storeys and with extensive well-developed gardens. Peacocks preened themselves as a couple of deer watched uninterestedly. Ali, the gardener, was watering the plants, paying particular attention to the hibiscus, his favourite. The red soil had darkened and gave off a 'just rained' smell as he aimed the hose at separate areas of the garden. A fresh breeze from the Indian Ocean made the plants sway slightly.

Under a shady tree, in an outdoor conservatory, Amina was braiding her younger sister Ayaan's hair. She loved this time of the evening, not only because it was cooler but because her beloved father would be coming home soon from work. He was the Governor of the Bank of Somalia and a member of the Marehan, the ruling clan. In fact, General Mohamed Siad Barre, the President, was his uncle. This afforded the family a special status and prestige known to few.

'Ouch,' wailed Ayan, as Amina pulled a little too tightly on her hair.

'Don't be a baby; you're ten,' scolded Amina as she continued braiding her hair. At fifteen, she did consider Ayan a baby, though.

At exactly six-thirty, Amina heard the heavy wrought-iron gates being opened by the two watchmen who kept guard on the house, and a sleek black Mercedes drove through. The driver, Omar, opened the back door, and her father stepped out.

Hair braiding forgotten, both Amina and Ayan ran forward to greet their father.

In an expensive Italian blue suit, Mohamed Abdi was at least six foot four inches tall, slim, and very handsome. Not thanking or even glancing at the driver, he stepped out of the car as his daughters hugged him. 'Hello girls,' he smiled, 'have you been good girls today?'

'We're always good, Dad,' they replied simultaneously.

He was very proud of his daughters. Several of his clansmen had encouraged him to take a second wife because his wife had only borne daughters, but he refused to do so. 'Well, maybe when she has a third child, it will be

What Will Be

a boy,' they said sympathetically. 'We only wanted two children, and we've got them, and they're healthy, thank God,' was Mohamed's usual reply.

What would they say if they knew that his wife Sahra could not have more children due to his vasectomy? He knew some of them thought he was not a man because he had not fathered a son, but he wasn't bothered by that. 'Let them think what they want, ignorant bastards, I'm happy with what Allah gave me,' he always told his wife.

Mohamed and his daughters walked the short distance to the house, and as soon as they walked in through the door, a maid appeared out of nowhere to take his briefcase and offer him a chilled glass of grapefruit juice. He took it without a word and sipped it as she put his slippers out for him.

He stepped out of his shoes and left them for the maid to silently collect and put away, not to be seen till the next morning, polished and shiny.

He took the stairs up to his room, greeted his wife and went to the bathroom for a shower. A few minutes later, he was out, feeling cool and relaxed. He put on a fresh vest and tied his macaawis, the Somali sarong, around his slender waist.

He went down the stairs to the dining room, a large ornate room dominated by what Amina always thought was an ugly mahogany table. Amina, Ayan and their mother were already seated at the table. As soon as he sat down, the maid appeared with a bowl of warm water and a towel, which she passed first to Mohamed, then to Sahra and finally to the girls. When they had all washed and dried their hands, another maid arrived and started putting various dishes on the table, all steaming hot from the kitchen.

The highly spiced goat curry smell was intoxicating, followed by saffron rice, various salads, and fruits. No meal was complete without anjelo, the Somali pancake that can be eaten sweet or savoury.

'Come on, tuck in before it gets cold,' said Sahra, and everyone started to help themselves.

Amina loved this time with her family, especially as her father usually regaled them with funny stories from the office. Today, however, he seemed a bit subdued. 'How was school today?' he asked his daughters.

'Same as always, Dad, boring!' answered Ayan.

'You must stop saying the school is boring, Ayan,' he said. 'Education is everything; without it, you will amount to nothing.'

What Will Be

'Plus, you're lucky,' Amina reminded her. 'You know most of our female cousins are not allowed to go to school.'

'Keep reminding her of that, Amina,' her mother said. 'Also, that she has such a nice father, otherwise, I would be grooming her for marriage!'

'But I'm only ten,' said Ayan. 'Ten-year-olds don't get married.'

'In this family, they don't, but other girls your age have already been promised to a man.'

'I still don't understand why the girls are not allowed to go to school, Mum. You and Dad are always telling us how important it is to get an education.'

'It's cultural, Amina. Many men believe a woman's place is in the kitchen. Education will spoil the girl, making her disrespectful and immoral. It's complete nonsense, of course, but that's what some people believe.'

'It's also a power thing,' said her dad. 'By keeping the girls ignorant, the men can control and manipulate women.'

'I think girls should all go to school and get an education, Dad.'

'Of course, I do too, and so does your mother.'

'Then why don't you talk to the uncles about our girl cousins and convince them to let them go to school?'

'They don't want me to interfere, besides I've already talked to them about that, and they think I'm mad for letting you two go to school!'

'You're not mad, Dad; you're just the best father in the world!'

'Keep remembering that,' Mohamed said with a laugh.

Ayan, listening attentively all this time, suddenly piped up, 'OK, OK, I get it. I won't ever say school is boring anymore, I promise.' She was still young enough to believe her mother's playful threats and definitely did not want to be married off at any age.

'Dad, anything funny happened at work today?' Amina asked.

'I wish there was,' he said, as he scooped some rice and curry with his hand and brought it to his mouth.

'Why, what's the matter?' asked Sahra anxiously.

'Well, it might just be rumours, but I heard that SNM {Somali National Movement} is causing trouble again. And the stupid Ethiopians are helping them to destabilise Uncle Siad's government.'

What Will Be

'What do these Amharas know?' said Sahra dismissively.

Amina knew from school that Amharas were a tribal group in Ethiopia. Still, Somalis have always used the word in a derogatory way.

'It's not only them,' Mohamed explained. 'It seems every clan in Somalia wants to form its own party and government. The Hawiyes have USC {United Somali Congress}, and the Ogadenis have SPF {Somali Patriotic Front}. Apparently, they seem to resent the fact that there are so many of our clan in government, but let's face it, what do they know? We're smarter than they are; most of them have never even seen the inside of a school! I mean, look at the Ogadenis; they'll only ever be soldiers, used by everyone. Can you imagine one of them in a powerful position in government? Allah protect us from them! I've been told there's fierce fighting going on in several parts of the country, and some of the rebels want to take Mogadishu. How they can even think of running the country is beyond me.'

Sahra agreed with her husband but had always maintained that clannism would be the end of Somalia. There had always been rivalries between the various clans. Still, until now, they had all managed to live peacefully together as one nation. She couldn't understand this; weren't they people with a common language, culture, and religion? Why couldn't people just get on?

Both Amina and Ayan had switched off; they did not like it when their father talked about serious stuff at the dinner table. They ate their dinner in silence, not understanding what their parents were talking about.

After dinner, the family retreated to the television room, decorated in Arabic style, with low seating, luxurious carpets and large, silk cushions. Here the maid would bring tea and dessert as they watched television or a video. If they felt like it, they would later drive to the corniche, park the car, and take in the evening breeze like most Mogadishu citizens. This was also a popular meeting place for friends and groups of young men furtively eyeing up the beautiful girls strolling leisurely along, leaving behind trails of perfume and unsi, the Somali incense.

Ice-cream vendors did a roaring business as they were the first port of call for families with children, as did sellers of sweets and small cakes. Sweet, spiced teas and coffees competed fiercely with the Arabian perfume aromas. The family didn't know it yet, but their lives were about to change forever.

Chapter 2

Not far from the city, the bedraggled rebel army of hungry and vicious men advanced. Their leader, his hair long and matted into a Rastafarian style, clutched a large bundle of qat, the drug of choice, in his hand. Qat looks quite innocent, just a bundle of green leaves with red stalks. In fact, it is a powerful narcotic used throughout East Africa and the Middle East. It is so powerful that it inhibits hunger and sleep and can cause euphoria and excitement. Men and women chew qat socially in homes across the country, usually in spacious, perfumed rooms. The drink of choice when indulging is Coca Cola or spicy, sugary black tea. Chewing gum and mints are also widely available.

The leaves are torn off and stripped from the bark, then stuffed in the mouth, chewed, and the juices sucked out. Users keep adding to it, not spitting it out, and just holding the contents in the corner of the cheek.

The rebel leader had such a big wad in his mouth that it gave him the appearance of a puffed fish. 'We'll take Mogadishu tomorrow,' he told his men, 'and get that Marehan dog Barre out of the palace. He's been there long enough. Let's rest tonight; we're gonna need all our strength tomorrow.'

They laid down their AK-47s and prepared to sleep. This was not easy; hunger pangs would stop them from getting a good night's sleep, not forgetting the qat that would interfere with their sleep.

Their leader had given each one a bundle to take the edge off the hunger. They talked among themselves well into the night. 'Hey man, did you hear about the big villas they have in Mogadishu?' asked one.

'Yeah,' answered another, 'and who lives there, man? The president's people. They say the rest of the country is suffering, but his people are getting richer and richer and live in these villas.'

'Just as well, we ran away from his army and joined with the Hawiye who are giving us more money. Everyone agrees that he hasn't been good to us, he's done nothing for any of us, and we always ate rotten food and slept outside like animals.'

'At least our own clansmen have promised us a better future.'

What Will Be

'All I can say,' said another brandishing his gun, 'is that revenge will be sweet. Very sweet.'

The next morning, the city woke to gunfire.

Chapter 3

At Mohamed Abdi's house, the family had also been woken up by the noise and gunfire. Amina and Ayan ran terrified into their parents' room and found Mohamed and Sahra already up.

Ali, the gardener, had just alerted the couple. He was usually the first up because he couldn't go back to sleep after the dawn prayer at five. As he came out of his quarters, he was surprised to see that the gate was wide open and there was no sign of the guards. He could hear the gunfire and screams as he walked out and looked up and down the road. Just then, a guard from the neighbouring house ran past and said, 'Brother, what are you standing there for? Run for your life; they're coming this way!'

'Who is?' asked Ali, shaken.

'The people who have taken over the country. Siad Barre has run away. Save yourself. Leave now!'

Ali had been with the family a very long time; he was practically family. He knew a takeover would not be good for his 'family', so he had run in and told Mohamed what he had heard.

'Just what I was saying last night,' said Mohamed, not very concerned.

'I'm sure it will ride over. Uncle will quash it soon.'

'They say he is gone, sir,' Ali replied.

Mohamed could not imagine or believe that. His uncle, a general, would never run away; there had to be another explanation. Nevertheless, he told Sahra to get their passports and start packing. If anarchy descended, he would save his family and put them on the first flight out of Mogadishu. Sahra quickly got out her vanity case and was stuffing cash and gold into it.

The gunfire got louder and louder and closer and closer to the house. Amina and Ayan were very scared, 'what's happening, Dad, where we are going?'

'Don't worry, we'll be alright,' said Mohamed unconvincingly. Being a general's nephew, he knew that the first point of call is usually the television and radio stations, the only way to communicate with the frightened and desperate masses in a coup.

Knowing this, he had turned on the radio. He heard the rebels boasting about taking over the country and finally kicking Barre out of Somalia.

What Will Be

The country was now theirs. 'Get the others to man the gates, now Ali!' he commanded.

'I'm sorry, sir, but there's no one at the gates; they've all run away,' said Ali.

'Rats! After all, I've done for them!' he said, furious. 'Has my driver Omar gone too?' he asked.

'Yes, sir.'

'That's fine. I'll drive us. Ali, go get your things; you're coming with us.'

Ali humbled that the family wanted to take him too, went to his quarters to collect his meagre belongings.

The servants' quarters are located at the back of the villas, hidden from view. As Ali bent to retrieve his prayer mat, he heard voices and more gunfire. 'Please Allah, let us be safe,' he prayed. He was about to return to the main house with his luggage when he saw ten rough-looking men waving AK-47 guns enter the compound. 'Oh God preserve us, they're here,' and he swiftly ducked back into his quarters.

'Just look at this, fellas,' one of the rebels said. 'See how Siad Barre's family lives. It's a good thing the neighbour told us who lives here. His nephew, if you please, the Governor of the Bank of Somalia!'

'Shoot that deer,' quick, that's our lunch,' he said as another took aim and ended the life of one of the deers who had been a family pet, patted and fed for years by the girls and Ali. At the sound of the shot, Mohamed and Sahra looked out of their window and were shocked at what they saw. One of the men had already slit the throat of the deer and was disembowelling it. He cut it into pieces and passed it around. 'Eat, my brothers,' he said. 'We'll need all our strength to empty this house!'

Sahra looked on mesmerised; she had heard that Amharas ate raw meat. Still, these were Somalis, speaking Somali but tearing into raw, bloody meat.

Amina and Ayan came to the balcony and started screaming hysterically when they saw what the men were eating. At that point, the rebels all grabbed their guns and got ready to fight. They had seen no one at the gate and had assumed the Governor had already fled, a coward just like his uncle. 'They're upstairs; let's go get them, bloody Marehans,' said one.

What Will Be

Four of them raced up the stairs, while the rest remained downstairs, taking what they thought was valuable and destroying what was not.

'Lock the door!' shouted Mohamed frantically to Sahra. 'Girls, come away from the balcony, now!' He tried the phone, but it wasn't working, the line must have been cut.

He went to his safe and withdrew the small pistol he had been given by his uncle as a gift. 'We have enemies,' he said. 'You never know when you might use it.'

How right he was, thought Mohamed as he heard the men pounding up the marble stairs. As Ali hadn't locked the door downstairs, it was easy for the men to get into the house. 'Hey, look at this, it's a small palace, but I bet his uncle's is bigger,' laughed one as he kicked an antique lamp to smithereens.

Soon they were at the bedroom door where Mohamed and his family huddled together, frightened. They started pounding loudly on the heavy door. 'We know you're hiding in there. Open the door, you bastard, or we'll break it.' Mohamed wasn't going to open the door, let them sweat. He wasn't a general's nephew for nothing. He would fight them to the end to protect his family.

He turned to look at his family; they were all crying and clearly very frightened. 'Remember, whatever happens here today, I love you all. Be strong and always look after each other,' he said, which made them cry even more.

The pounding on the door continued, until one of the rebels, in a spark of genius, shouted, 'Hey, we've got guns. Shoot the bloody door open. With any luck, we'll have shot them too.' A hail of bullets went through the door, creating small, round holes.

A few more kicks and the door swung open, and the rebels spilt into the large bedroom. Mohamed stood, arms protectively wide, his wife and daughters cowering behind him, his weapon concealed in his pocket.

The men took in the opulence of the room with its silk curtains and Egyptian cotton bed sheets. Even with their untrained and ignorant eyes, they could tell the fabrics weren't cheap. On the bed was the vanity case which Sahra had stuffed with money and jewellery. One of them immediately went for it and said to the others, 'Look at this, we're rich, boys. This will last us a long time.'

What Will Be

'Don't touch my things, you dirty dog!' Sahra said as she moved towards her case. Although she was scared, she was disgusted that this dirty and dishevelled man could actually be in the same room as her and have the gall to touch her case.

'What did you say, you filthy whore?' asked the evilest looking of the lot as he dragged Sahra from behind her husband and gave her a stinging slap. Tears sprang to Sahra's eyes as the two girls wailed and clung tighter to their father.

The others laughed and pointed their guns at the family.

'You think you are better than me? Do you think you have a God-given right to look down on me? Answer me, you daughter of a whore!' he screamed at Sahra, his eyes wild and bloodshot from too much qat, lack of food and sleep and God knows what else. As he pressed his face closer to hers, she noticed how much he stank and recoiled in disgust, almost gagging.

Suddenly, he grinned, revealing black stumps of what remained of his teeth, looking blacker against the pink of his gums. 'I'll show her that I'm better than the men in her clan, including him,' he said, pointing at Mohamed. He dragged her to the bed and threw her roughly on it.

Knowing what was going to happen, Sahra started praying and reciting verses of the Quran. 'Please Allah, protect me from these men.' She decided to appeal to the animal's human nature and started talking to him gently. 'Please, brother, do not hurt us. We have done nothing to you. Take my gold and anything else you want in the house, just please leave us alone, in the name of Allah, please leave us alone.'

'So now I'm your brother? Earlier I was a dirty dog, and you know what dogs do, don't you? They fuck bitches. Stop your yakking and take off your knickers.'

Sahra, sobbing, refused and one of the other rebels said, 'We'll give you a little help. You get her arms, and I'll get her legs.'

'There's no need to do that, please; her children are here,' pleaded Mohamed. He couldn't let his wife be violated, he was the only man she had ever known, and he loved her too much to let another man touch her.

'Who cares about your children? They will grow up hating and despising us as much as you do anyway,' said the one with the blackened teeth.

What Will Be

While one rebel held Sahra's arms in a tight grip, he pushed up her baati, the traditional kaftan Somali women wore both day and night and, to his delight, found she was wearing no knickers. He unzipped his dirty fatigues and pushed himself into her.

Sahra screamed as the other men laughed hysterically. Mohamed told his daughters to close their eyes and not to open them until he told them to. 'Am I not better than your husband?' asked the rebel, only to be met by silent sobbing.

'Give us a chance man,' the others said as the second rebel climbed up on top of Sahra. Mohamed could take no more. 'You are animals, you behave like animals, no, that is an insult to animals, you're worse. You're just depraved, godless monsters! No decent Somali man would do what you are doing. Fear your God, for you will surely be punished for this. You will go straight to hell.'

Mohamed slowly retrieved his gun from his pocket and shot the man dead just as he climaxed. As he did so, the others, stunned for a moment, suddenly opened fire on him. As he slumped to the floor, Amina and Ayan, shocked, stood rooted to the spot, unable to move or scream. Sahra pushed the corpse off her and ran to her husband, tears streaming down her face. 'You have killed him, you bastards. You have orphaned my children.'

The gun Mohamed used was by his side, and in a fit of anger and grief, Sahra grabbed it to shoot anyone of them; she didn't care which one. She had never held a gun before, and as she took aim, one of the men shot her straight in the eye. She collapsed without a sound next to her husband. 'Let's get out of here; this isn't the only targeted house in this street. Besides, we're finished here,' the rebel leader ordered.

'What about them, shouldn't we shoot them too?' asked one, gesturing toward Amina and Ayan.

'Leave them. They have to fend for themselves now and will probably not last the night. I'm sure other soldiers will pass through this villa, and we have a list of other houses to go to,' said the other, his mouth still bloody from the raw meat he had eaten.

They re-joined their friends downstairs and, laden with loot, left the now wrecked house of Mohamed Abdi.

As curious and anxious people strayed out of their homes to take a look, the rebels of USC {United Somali Congress} wreaked havoc on Mogadishu, a once beautiful ancient city. People were shot point-blank, mothers running back into their homes were shot in the back, those too shocked to move faced a barrage of bullets as smoke and wails engulfed the city. Some of the lucky ones were asked which clan they belonged to and, if they said Hawiye, were spared.

As chaos ensured, the news spread like wildfire through the city's neighbourhoods. USC had taken the capital and killed people. Those who had weapons at home started using them too, as clan against clan, neighbour against neighbour turned on one another. The ensuing bloodbath would never be forgotten. It is claimed that Hawiye women would spit on, and stab with a knife, a non- Hawiye who had already been shot to make sure they were dead. Such savagery by women was something never before seen in Somalia. The President, meanwhile, had left the country, leaving his countrymen to crucify each other. His palace, named Villa Somalia, was completely destroyed by the rebels, each falling brick symbolising the hatred they felt for him.

If the Hawiyes thought that their man Mohamed Ali Mahdi, who was to replace the exiled president, would bring stability, prosperity, and peace to the country, they were sadly mistaken. The Abgals and Habargedir, their own sub-clans, failed to agree on ruling as they fought each other. The warlords then split the capital into two, with Ali Mahad of the Abgal clan ruling the north and General Mohamed Farah Aideed of the Habargedir clan claiming the south. Mogadishu and indeed Somalia would never be the same again.

As the country descended into lawlessness, the UN, embassies, and other aid agencies left the country quickly and allowed the citizens to further destroy themselves and their country.

Chapter 4

Ali, who had hidden in fear in his quarters all this, time heard them leave and now peered out to see if it was safe to go into the main house. He couldn't believe the state of his beautiful garden. All his lovely plants were pulled up, his favourite hibiscus strewn all over. The remains of the deer lay next to the rose bush.

He had spent many years cultivating the garden and watering his plants, yet now it looked a deserted undergrowth. He walked past broken garden furniture as he made his way to the house.

What he saw when he entered the house was even worse. The beautiful curtains had been pulled down and ripped up, the expensive sofas also ripped open, precious lamps were broken, and televisions cracked and lying on the floor.

The house's ground floor looked like a bombsite; he could not believe that ten men could reduce such a magnificent house to a derelict site in a few minutes. He slowly climbed the stairs, noting the broken frames along the way, and when he got to the top, he called out quietly, 'Sir, Madam, it is Ali. They have gone.'

He hoped they were safe. Getting no answer, he stopped at their bedroom door, hesitating. He had never been in there; should he dare go in? He knocked loudly and, hearing nothing, pushed the door open.

The sight that greeted Ali broke his heart and was one that he would never forget. On the floor lay Mohamed, his shirt stained red, and next to him, his wife Sahra, her eyes still wide open, in a pool of blood. On the bed was a dead rebel, his red blood contrasting sharply against the white bedsheet. 'Oh Allah, have mercy on them,' he said.

Just then, he thought of the girls and started panicking. Where were they? 'Amina! Ayan!' he called hysterically, but as he looked around the room, he saw them, saw both of them standing still, arms around each other, trembling, eyes glued to their parents' corpses. It looked like they hadn't moved a muscle since their parents were killed, rooted, wide-eyed to one spot. 'Thank God you're alive. Come, we must get away from here,' he said, holding his hand out to the girls, who shrank back in fear. 'Oh God, what they must have been through,' he thought sadly.

What Will Be

He stepped closer to them and put his arms around them gently, and it was at this point that the flood of tears came for both Amina and Ayan. 'Ali, they killed Mum and Dad; they shot them in front of us.'

Their parents' bodies still lay where they fell, and now both girls flung themselves on their parents, sobbing uncontrollably.

'What will happen to us now? Who will look after us now, Amina?' asked Ayan. As the youngest, she immediately conferred leadership duties to her older sister.

'You can't stay here for sure. We have to go now; those soldiers might come back,' said Ali.

'But what about mum and dad? We can't just leave them here,' said Amina, feeling suddenly responsible and grownup.

'Yes, of course, we have to do something,' he said. 'According to our religion, the dead have to be buried within twenty-four hours, and it is our duty, us remaining three, to do that. While I see to a grave, collect whatever you need from your home quickly, and be ready to leave. I will call you out when I'm done.'

He went down the stairs to his quarters and got a hoe. He found a suitable place in the garden and started digging furiously. If the rebels came back and found him digging, they would surely kill him and dump him in the grave.

When he had dug a deep enough hole, he went back upstairs to retrieve his employers' bodies. He found the girls still in the bedroom, too frightened to venture out. 'Amina, can you find me two white sheets, please? I need them to wrap up your parents.'

Still sobbing, she went to her mother's linen cupboard and brought out the pristine cotton sheets that the maids used to wash, then iron perfectly. She silently handed them to Ali. He rolled Sahra off her husband and wrapped her in one of the sheets, 'Oh Allah, forgive me,' he thought. He knew he shouldn't be doing this, women should be doing this, and the body hadn't even been prepared for burial the Islamic way. Under normal circumstances, women would wash, shave, and scent Sahra's body for burial before being wrapped up in the white sheets. He couldn't very well ask the two young girls to do it for their mother; they had been traumatised enough.

What Will Be

When he finished wrapping up Sahra, he wrapped Mohamed up in the sheets. He lifted Sahra and, with great difficulty, put her on his shoulder and slowly carried her down the stairs. He was sweating copiously, what with her weight, rigor mortis and the heat.

He put the body in the grave and went back for Mohamed. 'Did you get your things together? After this, we really must go.'

They didn't know what to take; they had never packed or fended for themselves before. Their mother and the servants always took care of mundane tasks like that for them.

He understood they were afraid to leave the room, so he asked to escort them to their rooms to collect their things. They agreed eagerly, first going to Amina's room where she crammed clothes and books into a suitcase, then going next to Ayan's, who did the same. They all went back to the parents' bedroom, where Ali had the laborious task of taking down the second corpse and the girls their suitcases. 'I know you're too young for this, girls, but you must come and say goodbye to your parents. It is important. This way, at least you also know where they are buried.'

The girls stood beside Ali, sobbing loudly. He asked them to raise their hands and recite the prayer for the dead. He asked the girls to throw the first handful of earth into the grave when he had finished. He then used the hoe again to shovel earth and cover the grave.

Both Ayan and Amina would never forget the sight of their parents, wrapped in white sheets, lying side by side in the grave. They sobbed uncontrollably, holding hands, and clinging to each other.

'You will see them in the afterlife,' Ali reassured them, giving the orphans what comfort he could. 'When we leave this house, you will cease to be Marehan. You will say you are Hawiye and don't mention your parents. There are bad people out there who will want to harm you just because of who you are. If they ask you who I am, say I am your uncle.'

As they walked out of the gates, Amina looked back, face wet with fresh tears, wondering if she would ever see her home again, the home that was now devoid of the loving parents they always took for granted. Mogadishu was now in the hand of lawless rebels.

Chapter 5

Amidst all the gunfire and mayhem, Ali managed to get the girls safely to his village outside the city. This was the baadiye, the countryside that the girls had always heard of but had never been to. They had often heard their parents and others putting down people from baadiye, saying that they were peasants who knew nothing; they had never seen a television or a radio in their lives or a car for that matter. Now here they were, away from the opulence of their life in the city to this.

The village was made up of a cluster of small mud huts. As they arrived, they were greeted by an entourage of naked children, both boys and girls, all curiously staring at these strange girls. Amina and Ayan were wearing jeans and tops, and their hair was uncovered, unheard of in the country. Girls their age wore a scarf to hide their hair and the guntino, a floor-length sari-like garment wrapped around the body and tied at one shoulder. On top of this, they threw a thin cotton scarf, goo, around their shoulders. More people came out of the huts; they had never seen people like these two girls. 'Are they boys, Uncle Ali?' inquired one little boy.

'They're girls whose parents have been brutally murdered in front of them. Their father, may Allah rest his soul in peace, was my employer, the best man and employer.'

'But why are they wearing boys' clothes?' asked another of the children.

Ali, used as he was to seeing the girls in their jeans, had forgotten the impact they would have here in his small village. 'That's how girls dress in Mogadishu. Leave them alone now,' he said as he led them quickly to his hut.

His wife was at the entrance to her house. Ali greeted her, and she quickly closed the door behind them as they all went in.

'These are my employer Mohamed's daughters. I had no choice but to bring them here. Mogadishu is burning, the rebels have taken over. Their parents were shot right in front of them, and their home was destroyed. I couldn't leave them; their parents have always been so good to me. They have no-one else now, except us.'

Habibo, a small, gentle woman who had not been blessed with children of her own, welcomed Amina and Ayan into her home. She brought them some sousaac, fermented camel milk to drink, and muqmadh, the dried camel meat, the Somali equivalent of biltong. They were used to spaghetti bolognese and pasta al forno, but they ate and drank what was offered because they were hungry. Ayan made a face as she tasted sousaac for the first time, she started to complain, but a stern look from her sister silenced her. Hence, she just pretended to enjoy the sour-tasting milk.

Inside, the hut was cool and quite large. In one corner was a makeshift bed, raised slightly off the ground for Habibo and Ali. On the floor was a woven straw mat and a large tin suitcase glinted in another corner. This contained Ali and Habibo's clothes and meagre linen.

'Ali, go to Adan and ask if he has a spare bed for the girls; they cannot sleep on the floor,' she said to her husband. She didn't want to scare the girls, but the beds were off the ground because of the snakes and scorpions that sometimes tried to share their beds.

She remembered her mother telling her that a snake had wound itself around her when she was a baby. Her father had to carefully remove it and strike it dead on the head. Perhaps that explained her phobia of snakes and other creepy crawlies.

Ali came back with Adan, who helped him put a bed in one corner of the hut. It was just a basic frame and slates made from timber and had a straw mattress. A white sheet with big red flowers and two thin grey blankets were deposited on the bed. There were no luxurious down pillows. Habibo gave them two more sheets and showed them how to roll them up and use them as makeshift pillows. 'Or you could use some of your clothes,' she suggested.

Behind the hut was a smaller one, which was the bathroom, except this had no roof. There was no running water, water had to be fetched from the well, which was an hour's walk away, and if one wanted a shower, one took a bucket of water and a bar of soap to the bathroom.

They didn't wash very often; water was too precious to waste. Also, there was no electricity, and the villagers used small kerosene lamps to light the way at night. There were no toilets; the villagers had to hide behind a bush to pee or poo and then bury the evidence or cover it with twigs or leaves. They carried plastic bottles with water to wash after; there was no such thing as toilet paper.

What Will Be

It was a completely new way of life for Amina and Ayan, although they settled in gratefully. There was no school, only the dugsi, the Islamic school where an old man taught the Quran to the children, wielding a thin stick to hit those who did not or would not learn their suras or verses by heart.

In the morning, the men and boys herded the goats, cows, and camels while the women and girls worked the fields and the homestead. Habibo coaxed the girls out of their jeans and gradually changed the way the girls dressed. After an unfamiliar and uncomfortable few weeks, they became experts at wearing their traditional Somali outfits and proudly showed off to each other.

Habibo became their mother figure, and they stayed close to her, never venturing far away from her. 'Ali, I have come to love these girls like they were my own,' she said to her husband one night. 'Can't they stay with us forever?'

'No, Habibo, you know they can't stay here forever. And I knew you would get attached to them; they are lovely children. I've known them since they were born and watched them grow, so I feel attached to them too. I have to find ways of getting them out of here. The villagers know they are not our daughters, we can't trust them not to betray us, and their parents' killers are still baying for Marehan blood. I owe it to their parents to get them as far away as possible from here. I have heard that many people are fleeing to Kenya, they say it is safer there, so I will make inquiries on my next visit to the city. So, just enjoy their company for now.'

So, she did. She taught them how to cook and sew and told them countless stories about the countryside and the people. Every night, she would make them laugh or cower with the bedtime stories that she told them. They loved going out with her when she gathered herbs and taught them how to use these same herbs as medicine. If any of them had a cough, she boiled some of these herbs and mixed them with honey, which soon put paid to the ailment. She also used to rub some strange green goo which she called 'my miracle mask' on their faces. 'It'll make your faces soft and smooth,' she told them. 'Don't forget, milk and honey are all you need to stay beautiful, my girls, inside and outside!'

Meanwhile, once a beautiful city dating back to the 13th century, Mogadishu burned, villas destroyed and looted, cars and property stolen or burned, the president long gone. But although the villagers heard all about it from people returning from the city, they remained untouched by the violence and chaos.

There was nothing to loot from them; everyone knew baadiye people didn't have much. They were self-sufficient, had food, and their livestock provided both milk and meat, the Somali staple diet.

Amina had made friends with one of the village girls, Cambaro, who was around her age. They spent days braiding each other's hair, talking, and laughing about everything. When Amina told her friend about her former life in Mogadishu, Cambaro could not believe any of it. She thought Amina was making it all up, telling her fancy stories. She had no idea what television was and laughed at her description of spaghetti. 'Amina, you can't seriously tell me you used to eat worms! As for tea, girls don't drink tea; only married women drink tea!'

Nevertheless, Amina continued telling her about her life, if only to remind herself of her other, past life.

'Have you had a period?' Cambaro asked her one day.

'No, what's that? Amina asked.

'Oh, it's when you bleed down below; it shows you're a woman then.'

'Have you had it?' she asked her friend.

'Yes, of course, so I'm a woman now, not a little girl.'

Amina's mother had never got around to telling her about this, and she felt a bit sad that this information had to be given to her by an illiterate village girl. That night, she asked Habibo about it, who told her everything she needed to know. 'You should be getting yours by now; let me know when you do. And don't worry, it's a natural and normal thing for girls your age.'

'Will I get it too?' asked Ayan anxiously.

'Yes, you will,' laughed Habibo, 'but only when you're a big girl. And don't look so worried; it's not an infectious disease!'

Chapter 6

The days passed by quietly, silently, almost happily. One day Cambaro said to her, 'I can't play with you any longer.'

'Why?' Amina wanted to know.

'Because soon I will be embarking on the next stage of womanhood, and you'll still be a child.'

'Are you going away? Amina asked sadly. She did not want her friend to go away.

'Don't be silly. I am not going anywhere. A few other girls and I are going to be circumcised.'

'What's that?' Amina asked, hating to sound so ignorant in front of her friend. She was the one from the city who had gone to a proper school, she should know about that and other different things.

'Are you telling me you don't know what circumcision is?' asked Cambaro incredulously. 'Don't tell me you city girls don't get circumcised. How will you ever find a husband?'

'Please tell me,' pleaded Amina.

'Well, they cut you down below and stitch you up.'

'What!!?' shrieked a horrified Amina. 'Who's they? And they can't do that!'

'They do, and yes, they can. You know that old lady who lives in the hut opposite us? She does it; she will cut us.'

'Aren't you afraid?' Amina asked her.

'No, my older sister had it done, but she won't tell me about it. But my mum says I have to be brave and not cry. If I don't do it, I will be the laughing stock of the village, and I will never be married.'

Amina ran once more for answers to Habibo, who was as surprised as Cambaro that Amina and her sister were not circumcised. 'Habibo, why do they do it?'

'It is our way,' she told Amina. 'Every Somali girl has to go through circumcision. I went through it, my mother before me and my grandmother before her. Even though the Holy Quran says girls should not be circumcised, only boys. The Arabs do what they call Sunna. They just cut the tip of the clitoris which I think is not proper circumcision.'

Although embarrassed by such talk, Amina wanted to know more, and Habibo was only too happy to oblige. 'What we Somalis do is better; we cut off the whole clitoris, followed by the lips of the vagina and then we sew them together, leaving a small hole for urination. This way, our girls are protected from being promiscuous because they have no clitoris, they can't get sexually excited and will remain virgins until their wedding day.'

'But that's barbaric!' Amina said.

Habibo could only say, 'It is our way.'

That night Habibo shared the shocking news with her husband. 'Ali, can you believe that the girls are not circumcised? At their age? What is this world coming to? Should I get them done?'

'Not under any circumstance. It is not your job to do that. Your job is to protect them, and that means even from circumcision!' Ali didn't really want to know all this; it was women's talk, so to stop her talking further about it, he said, 'It's no big deal anyway, some of the educated Somalis no longer circumcise their daughters. And remember, these two lost their parents at a crucial age, so please show a bit of sympathy.'

The next week, Cambaro was circumcised by the old lady and segregated to a separate hut from her family. She and the other two girls who shared her fate would stay there until they healed. Such operations were sometimes lethal, as in cases where an untrained circumciser cut into a vein, and a young girl's life was lost needlessly. There were no hospitals in the village. The nearest one was in Mogadishu, miles away. As a result, many young girls lost their lives before getting to the capital for treatment.

Amina missed her friend and ventured into the hut one day, only to find Cambaro, sullen and in pain. She took in the straw mats the girls were lying on, small plates of half-eaten food on the floor and a brown gourd of milk. Then she spotted Cambaro on the floor, a rope tied round her thighs. 'Why are you tied up like that? Are you OK?' Amina asked.

'What do you think?' Cambaro spat angrily. 'Do I look OK, sitting here, with a wound between my legs and a rope tied around me to make sure the stitches never come out? I have been butchered with a razor blade, it was so painful and the worst pain I ever endured in my life.'

What Will Be

'I'm so sorry Cambaro, how can I help?'

Suffering from pain, anger, and frustration, Cambaro hit back at her friend. 'You can help by getting out of here! Get out and go bore someone else with your big city stories. And don't come back!'

Amina fled, in tears, crying both for the end of her friendship and the injustice done to Cambaro. As usual, she went crying to Habibo, who hugged her, kissed her brow, and told her to forget about this, 'At least it won't happen to you or Ayan.'

That was a small comfort, but she vowed there and then that if she ever had a daughter, she wouldn't do this awful thing, and she would make sure that nobody did it to her and her sister. From now on, if anyone asked, she would lie and say they had both been circumcised. It was safer this way for both of them.

Not long after this incident, Ali came home one day and told Habibo that she had to pack whatever rations she could find for the girls because he had found someone to take them to Kenya.

Habibo was in tears, she did not want the girls to leave, but Ali insisted it was for their own safety.

She called the girls into the hut and told them what Ali had said with a breaking heart.

'Can't we just stay with you?' Ayan asked. In the time they had lived with her, they had become very close to her, and the idea of leaving what had now become their home was unbearable.

'No, sweetheart, I wish you could both stay with me forever, but you can't. Those bad men who killed your parents might still come here for you. We cannot trust every one of the villagers, and one of them might give your identity away for a price. So, it is safer that you go.'

'But where will we go, who will look after us?' cried Ayan.

'Don't worry, you will be safer anywhere other than here. I have heard that Kenya is a nice country, and they even have Somali people living there, good ones, not like the ones who live here. The ones living in Kenya have no concept of clannism; they see each other as only Somalis living in a foreign country. They love, respect and protect each other.'

It took a lot of convincing to make them believe another country was safer and better than their own, but, left with no choice, the sisters slowly accepted that for the second time in their young lives, they would have to leave home.

The sad atmosphere in the hut was alleviated by a visit from Cambaro, now recovered from her ordeal. 'Sorry I was so rude Amina, I was hurting and upset and just took it out on you. You are the same age as me, and there you were, happy and smiling while I was in agony. Still, it's over now, but please don't ask me to talk about it. Every girl has to experience this for herself, pretty much like childbirth.'

Amina was so overjoyed at the sight of her friend that she forgave her fully and immediately.

Although they still laughed and gossiped about everyone, Cambaro had changed. She was quieter and sometimes seemed distant. 'It's because she's a woman now,' Amina thought, 'and has to put foolish childhood antics behind her.' Still, she missed her friend of old, but life for her temporarily slipped back into normal. However, the impending doom of her and her sister leaving home never left her.

A month later, as Cambaro and the sisters walked back into the village from the well, they noticed a commotion at Cambaro's house. Several women were scurrying along, some with big cooking pots and others with bags of rice and meat. 'I wonder what's happening,' said Cambaro. 'Usually, those pots appear at big festivals like Eid or at weddings, births or funerals.'

'Do you think someone's died?' Amina asked fearfully. She had been frightened of death since witnessing her parents.

'Don't know, let's go find out.'

As the girls got closer to the hut, some women started ululating as soon as they saw Cambaro. Embarrassed, she turned to her mother and asked what was going on.

'Oh, my daughter, such a blessed day. You see, you are getting married today. Your father has accepted a proposal on your behalf from Uncle Abdirisak's family. You are marrying his son Adan, such a handsome boy!'

Amina and Cambaro stood where they were, rigid with shock.

'Get a move on, Amina, go with her to the next hut where women are waiting to get her ready for the wedding tonight.'

What Will Be

They were shoved in by a kindly aunt who told Cambaro not to worry; everything would be alright.

'But you are too young to get married, Cambaro,' Amina said. 'You're my age, and I would never marry now.'

'You!' responded one of the older aunts, 'don't put such nonsense into her head. She is not too young; she is at the right age. You should be getting married too.'

As soon as Amina heard this, she fled the hut and ran all the way to the safety of Habibo's arms. 'Why, Habibo, why?' she cried. 'And without any warning? She didn't even know she was getting married today! I remember my mother telling us that girls get married young in baadiye, but I didn't think so young.'

Through Ali, Habibo had known that this was an alien concept to her two girls, brought up in the city as they were. 'As I explained before, this is the way of life here, Amina,' she said gently. 'Her parents have chosen who they think is the right person for her; they wouldn't have done this lightly. Adan and his family would have been studied and observed for a long time, his ancestry checked, his behaviour too. It's good for Cambaro to get married. She will have a husband to look after her and soon, God willing, children for her to look after. She will have a good life here; she is not educated; her husband will provide for her. Be happy for your friend.'

The whole village turned up for the wedding, as there was never any need for an invitation. Weddings were always welcomed as there was plenty of food and merriment. Cambaro sat in one hut, dressed in the red and yellow bridal guntino, her head bowed and covered with a large, shiny, gold shawl. She had elaborate henna designs on her hands all the way, up to her elbows. On her feet, the same designs snaked their way up to her ankles. Heavy gold rings adorned her fingers, and numerous gold bangles jangled from her tiny wrists. Next to her sat her sister and her cousin. They were there to bring her food and drink, although, in true Somali tradition, she should not be seen eating or drinking on her wedding day, what with everyone watching her.

Women streamed into the hut, singing, and occasionally going up to the bride and kissing her and congratulating her. Inside the next hut sat her groom Adan, his male relatives and the Kadhi, the man who would marry them.

What Will Be

'How much is the mehr, the bride price?' the Kadhi asked the groom's father.

'Twenty camels and some gold,' he replied, which the Kadhi wrote down in Arabic on a piece of paper.

'And what is her name?'

'Cambaro Rashid.'

'Ah, yes, is that Rashid's eldest?'

'Yes.'

'Has she agreed to this marriage?'

'Her family has agreed, Kadhi, you know her father is my second cousin,' explained Adan's father.

'But according to Islam, the bride has to agree herself,' the Kadhi reminded him.

'Since when do we ask girls what they will or will not agree to Kadhi,' laughed the groom's father. 'Just get on with it and marry them now please.'

Without a fight, the Kadhi then wrote out the marriage certificate and gave it to Adan.

'Go tell the women it's done, Ahmed,' Adan's father said to his youngest son, who promptly went out and told the first woman he saw. She ululated very loudly and was soon joined by the others, beating drums, and dancing their way to Cambaro's hut. Inside, Cambaro, her sister and her cousin heard the commotion.

Her mother was first to enter, kissed her and said, 'You are officially a married woman now; they are coming to take you to your own home, where your husband will be waiting for you.'

Under the shawl, Cambaro sobbed silently. She did not want to be married, yet she was married and going to a home and husband she did not want. At that moment, she envied Amina. Amina had no parents to force her into wedlock, no parents to force her into female genital mutilation. Amina would be leaving soon, too, going to Kenya. At the same time, she would languish in baadiye for the rest of her life, herding goats and bearing children. She felt someone holding her hand and knew instantly it was Amina. She offered comfort and understanding without saying anything. When she was inside the marital hut, her shawl was removed from her head, and the first person she focused on was Amina, whose eyes were as red as hers.

What Will Be

Silently, the two hugged each other but were soon separated by the dancing, singing women. Cambaro started married life reluctantly and unhappily, and soon, Amina too would start a new life in exile.

Chapter 7

A week after the wedding, Amina and Ayan left the village, sobbing and heartbroken yet again. They had left behind their surrogate parents Ali and Habibo. They were equally heartbroken but relieved that the girls would be taken from Somalia to a safe country. Ali had found a woman who said she would take them as her daughters because she, too, was fleeing the country.

A military Land Rover arrived in the middle of the night to take them away from what they now thought of as home. Habibo had packed some camel meat and rice for them to eat on the journey. She had also given them a few hundred shillings, what she could afford to give, and told them to buy sodas and food with it. The driver was a silent and serious middle-aged man. Next to him sat an old man with bright red hair and beard, the result of dyeing white hair with henna. In the back sat the woman Anab, Amina and Ayan.

The old man fingered his rosary beads and offered prayers for a safe journey as they sped into the night. The two sisters held hands all night, even when they fell asleep.

The journey to Garissa, a town in northern Kenya populated mainly by Somalis, was over five hundred miles and would take nearly fourteen hours.

The Land Rover sped south throughout the night and was stopped only once at Jamaame, 225 miles from Mogadishu, by bandits, the ubiquitous AK-47s at the ready. High on qat, they peered into the vehicle to see who was in it and if they could get anything out of these travellers. Amina and Ayan started screaming when they saw the armed bandits, but Habibo put her arms around them and told them to stop it. 'You don't want to give them a reason to even look at you,' she said.

'Who are you and where are you going to at this hour of the night?' asked one.

The driver, who had no intention of telling them they were fleeing the country, came up with a well-rehearsed story. 'My name is Ahmed, brother, and this old man is my father, and the woman is my sister, and the girls are her daughters. I am taking them to visit my dying brother who lives in a village nearby; that's why we're travelling through the night.'

What Will Be

'Why are these girls crying?'

'They are very fond of their uncle, and every time he is mentioned, they dissolve into tears, that's all.' Cleverly, he continued, 'I can see you haven't eaten, brothers. Please take this food for yourselves, and although I don't have a lot of money, these 400 shillings should get you a decent breakfast tomorrow.' He handed over the food and the cash and was told to go on his way after another look inside the vehicle. Thankfully, they hadn't asked him what his clan was, and he knew he had got off lightly. He had heard of other drivers who were not so lucky, shot dead along with their passengers and the vehicles then set on fire.

Garissa, Kenya

Several hours later, tired, and hungry, they arrived in the North Eastern Province of Kenya or NFD as the local Somalis referred to it. The driver had told them most of the people here were Somali, and they would get food and shelter. He dropped them off in front of a gate surrounded by very high barbed wire. His job done, he bade them farewell and went off to find a place to sleep.

Bewildered, the small group stood by the side of the road, not knowing what to do or where to go.

An officious looking man walked up to them. 'You're new arrivals,' he stated as he looked them up and down, the old man, now looking even older, the woman, adjusting her thin shawl and the two young girls, thin and dirty. He has seen this repeatedly and was getting used to seeing these poor, dishevelled refugees arriving in a never-ending steady stream from Somalia. A Somali himself but born in Kenya, Hassan was an employee of the United Nations High Commission for Refugees, UNHCR, based in Dadaab.

This hot, dusty town had a refugee camp to home the many displaced people who arrived here daily in large numbers. He introduced himself, told them where they were and asked the little group to follow him. He then led them through the gates to a school desk and a couple of chairs under a tree, which he asked the old man and the woman to occupy. From an icebox next to him, he extracted four bottles of water and handed them out. 'First, I have to register you as refugees, then I will take you into the camp and give you your rations,' he said. He took their names, dates of birth if they knew it (the old man and the woman didn't know, so a date was bestowed upon them), but Amina gave hers and her sister's. When this was done, he led them into the camp, and the girls gasped in disbelief. They didn't want to live here. They had never seen anything like this in their lives. A sprawling mess of mud huts greeted their eyes, teeming with skinny, desperate looking people. The earth was cracked and dry and, on it, makeshift huts had been built or were in the process of being built. There was no greenery.

A few of the shelters were tents donated by the United Nations. Most were built out of twigs and covered with anything useful, such as plastic carrier bags and discarded bits of cloth. Surrounding this was barbed wire, designed to keep the refugees in and away from the rest of the town. Yellow and white plastic jerry cans containing water were visible everywhere while naked, malnourished children played outside their huts or simply lay on the floor, their bare legs ashen and scrawny.

Ayan began to cry and Amina, close to tears herself, told her to pull herself together. 'At least we're safe here; we won't be shot; remember what happened to our mum and dad.'

Hassan took pity on them and led them to a newly constructed hut. The four of them would share it. There were thin, threadbare mattresses on the floor and nothing else. Hassan said he would go and organise their monthly food ration and would be back with it momentarily. In the meantime, they should rest and get used to being in Kenya. Wearily, they each sat on a mattress, the only claim to a bed any of them would have for a long time. Not long after, Hassan appeared with small packets of rice, flour sugar, tea, a few tins of tomatoes and beans, as well as a jerry can of vegetable oil. He also brought a jiko, a Kenyan stove that uses charcoal and a few cooking utensils, four tin cups and plates and no cutlery save for one wooden serving spoon. He dumped these in a corner and left. 'I'm going to try and get you some lunch, but this is only for new arrivals, so don't expect it every day. From tomorrow you will have to cook for yourselves.'

'I wonder if the food he's going to get us will be halal,' mused the old man.

'We were told that many Somali people live here, so I'm sure it will be halal,' said the woman, 'in any case, that's the least of our worries, and we have to eat it whether it's halal or not. Otherwise, we will die.

'Now that we have been placed together, we should introduce ourselves properly. I am Anab, and I come from a little town just outside Mogadishu. My granddaughters, what are your names?' the old man asked.

What Will Be

Amina answered, 'Amina and Ayan. We are sisters, and we are from Mogadishu.'

'My name is Farah,' said the old man, and I come from Baidoa.' Ordinarily, he wouldn't have shared a room with a woman other than his wife, but for now, he was grateful to be sharing. He was old and frail, and he knew that the woman and the two girls would look after him. 'As the oldest one here, please show me your respect by not asking me or each other what clan we belong to. Remember, it is due to this clan rivalry that we are here, miles away from our homes and in someone else's country. We have been thrown together by cruel fate, but we are all the family we have now, and so we must present a united front and look after each other.'

They all agreed, and soon after, Hassan arrived with lunch, white rice, and some sort of stew, and the four ate in silence. Still tired from the long journey, they soon succumbed to sleep.

Amina woke up in the middle of the night, cold, stiff, and uncomfortable. It was pitch-black, and she could hear Farah snoring loudly. Wondering what time it was, she thought longingly of her simple bed in Habibo's house and how she felt safe and loved there. Here she felt like an animal, no clean clothes, no warm bed, no hot food and not even a door. Anyone could walk in.

Her stifled sob woke her sister up, and she heard her frightened voice, 'Amina, are you there?'

'Yes, I'm here. Shall we go and talk outside the hut so we don't wake the others?'

They stepped out and looked around. The camp was silent, not a soul about, the only noise coming from the rustling of bushes blown away by the night wind.

'We'll be OK, Ayan, don't worry, let's just be strong for each other. That's what mum and dad would have wanted.'

'Do you think they're in heaven, Amina?'

'Of course, they are, and they are watching over us. Look at the sky.' The sky was black with a million glittering, silver stars and so enchanting that for a moment, the girls forgot where they were and stood silently staring at the sky until Amina suggested they go back to sleep. Holding hands, they silently slipped back into the hut and groped their way to Amina's mattress.

What Will Be

This is where Anab found them, arms around each other when she woke up early for prayers.

The next morning, they were woken up by people talking loudly, children playing, pots clanging and water splashing. They peered outside and saw that Anab was already up and outside the hut, squatting over the jiko. She was cooking angelo for everyone, and Farah was sitting on a makeshift stool next to her. 'Good morning girls, come and have breakfast. You will need your strength around here.' They sat on the floor and devoured the sticky pancake, dripping with oil and covered in sugar. They were so hungry, Anab had to keep the pancakes coming until, mouths and fingers greasy, the girls indicated they had had enough. 'Just as well you're full; we have to watch our rations,' she laughed. 'Well, we have the whole day ahead of us, with nothing to do, so go and explore, but don't go too far out.' She was already acting, the mother thought Amina as she dragged Ayan away.

Old men in maacawis, the traditional Somali sarong, sat outside the huts observing the comings and goings of the people. They were cleaning their teeth with caadhey, a twig from the acacia tree, which for years had been the only means of cleaning teeth by the nomadic Somalis.

A few old ladies had mats outside their huts, on which skinny babies and toddlers rolled. 'Ayan, do you know that the caadhey is supposed to be better than a brush and toothpaste?'

Amina asked. 'Really?'

'Yes, apparently it has antiseptic and anti-bacterial properties and people who use them never get cavities.'

'Then why didn't we use them at home?'

'Because we are city folk, stupid. Only people from baadiye, the bush use them.'

'Are all these people from the bush, Amina?'

'How should I know? That man Hassan said they are all refugees from Somalia, so I'm sure some of them are from the bush.'

No one bothered them as they wandered around the camp until they saw a group of children under a tree in whose midst sat an old man of around seventy. He looked up at the girls with rheumy eyes, the irises of his black eyes turning blue from age or undiagnosed cataracts. 'Come and join us,' he

What Will Be

invited kindly. 'This is dugsi where you children will learn the Holy Quran so that you don't forget your religion and your culture.'

Ayan looked inquiringly at Amina, who said, 'Let's do it! It's not as if we have anything else to do, and it might kill a few hours. Otherwise, we'll die of boredom!'

Chapter 8

Gradually, the girls settled into a routine. After breakfast and helping Anab clean the hut, it was straight to dugsi for three hours. Then it was time for a small lunch of rice or barley with milk, after which they either went for a siesta or just sat outside the hut playing with a twig and using it to draw designs on the dry earth. They had met other girls close to their ages, Qamar, named after the moon, with a perfectly round moon face and a small mouth, Shukri who looked stupid with big vacant frog's eyes, her mouth always hanging open and Istanbul, beautiful and named after the Turkish city even though her parents had no idea where it was. Amina didn't want to challenge her directly. Still, she thought it was stupid naming girls after cities, especially as the Somalis always got the pronunciation wrong. Paris became Bariis, and Sterling became Istarrlin, rendering the meaning completely different. Bariis was close to baris, the word for rice in the language. She wished they would just stick to Somali names or at least Islamic names. She remembered how her father always said Somali names were the most beautiful, just like Somali girls were the most beautiful in the world. How she still missed him and her sweet, gentle mum.

One night several weeks later, Amina woke up with crippling stomach pains and a feeling of wetness between her legs. 'I must be dying,' she thought as she hobbled over to her sister.

'What's the matter,' a sleepy Ayan asked her.

'I think I'm ill, my tummy hurts, and it feels wet down.... you know.... below.'

'I don't know what to do; we should wake Anab,' who was already stirring from her sleep due to the girls' whispers.

'What is it, girls? Go back to sleep.'

'Amina is dying,' Ayan said tearfully, and Anab quickly stood up and rushed over to them. She asked Amina where it hurt and when Amina described her symptoms, Anab laughed, which baffled the sisters. 'It's O.K, you're not dying, and you've just had your first period. From now on until you get to your fifties, may Allah keep you that long; you will bleed every month for a few days. You are becoming a young woman, so make sure you do not go near boys.'

Amina told her Habibo had already told her about periods and not to go near boys. 'Will I bleed too?' a frightened Ayan asked. 'Yes, you will, Ayan but not yet.'

Anab made Amina go outside to wash, then gave her some rags. She instructed Amina to put these inside her knickers a makeshift sanitary pad. 'I will see tomorrow morning if I can get you proper sanitary pads from some of the other women.'

Amina's period was the topic of discussion the next day amongst her friends. 'Welcome to the club,' said Qamar, 'mine started last year. You do know you can't go to dugsi until your periods are over.'

'No, I didn't know that; why?'

'Because you can't touch the Quran in your state,' added Bariis. 'Personally, I relish the days not going to dugsi. It gives me a break from not being hit by that maalim every time I get a surah wrong.'

'Do you use sanitary pads? Anab said she'd find me some.' Amina said, and they all laughed.

'Sanitary pads? That's a luxury we can't afford here. I didn't even know what they were until Istarrlin's mum showed me one that she somehow got from a white woman who visited the camp one year. We all use rags cut off from old bits of baati that our mothers discard because they have holes and cannot be worn anymore,' explained Qamar.

For two years Amina and her sister endured the refugee camp. Along the way, the old man Farah passed away. He wasn't missed much, as he never had anything to say and always just waited for Anab and the two sisters to cater to his daily needs. God knows what clan he belonged to because he certainly didn't go out of his way to be the family member that Anab and the girls yearned for. He was always polite, said good morning and goodnight but wasn't interested in his fellow hut occupants. He just ate whatever was put in front of him, without thanks to Anab, who now had to toil to get charcoal for the jiko and create delicious meals out of the small monthly rations allocated to them.

The sisters remembered his last day when the men came to take him away for burial. His body was washed and wrapped in a clean white burial

What Will Be

sheet. Verses of the Holy Quran were read over the body, after which it was carried away by the men. Anab was visibly upset, although he was no relation of hers. He was taken away to a burial area in the camp, and no one would hear or talk of Farrah anymore. He had died a paupers' death, poor, alone and with not one member of his family present.

The sisters had tried to relate to him and tried to make him into a granddad figure, but it hadn't worked; he simply wasn't interested. Still, they were sad he had gone; he had been with them through the arduous journey from Somalia to Kenya. It was only the three of them now, and Anab had slowly established herself as the sisters' new surrogate mother. They were only too happy to have a mum and loved her and respected her as such. After all, they had no one apart from her at the camp, as they had no family; she was the one they regarded as family.

The sisters never spoke of what happened to them or their family in Somalia. They were still so traumatised and shocked that it was buried deep inside, and neither wanted to discuss the topic. It was easier to ignore it and pretend it never happened. Whenever the other girls asked about their parents, they ignored the questions or simply evaded them by saying they didn't remember much from their life in Mogadishu.

Almost everyone, however, had similar stories to tell of rape, pillage, and theft of property. It was what brought some of them closer and some of them further apart. Minor disagreements were a regular occurrence among the refugees, especially when one insulted a particular clan. However, before escalating into a full-scale war, self-appointed elders intervened. The elders, just by their great age, were respected by all. 'It was clan fighting that destroyed our country and forced us to live in this Godforsaken place, don't bring the war to us,' they often pleaded. Sometimes their words weren't heeded, and men stabbed each other fatally. It became common to see Kenyan doctors at the camp, just as it was seeing the group of men carrying corpses away for burial in the cemetery.

At the age of seventeen, Amina had grown into a beautiful young woman. She had big brown eyes with long jet-black lashes, and her thick, braided hair hung below her shoulders.

Ayan, at twelve, had also grown, quicker than her sister. She had developed breasts which Amina was envious of and had also grown taller.

What Will Be

Qamar once told Amina that the young men in the camp had begun noticing Ayan.

'Rubbish, she's too young,' protested Amina.

'Oh yeah? Watch what happens next time we walk past them.'

'Why wait? Let's put it to the test now, then you'll see you're mistaken.' She called out to Ayan, who walked slowly towards her. She loved her big sister because she let her stay with her friends even though the other girls thought she should join girls her age. Just the other day, she heard Baris say, 'We can't talk about boys or anything grown-up with her listening in. Really, she should hang around girls her own age and play hopscotch or whatever.'

Amina never listened to them because she always wanted her sister by her side. 'We're going for a walk; come with us,' she said to a delighted Ayan.

The huts in the camp were arranged in a circle, so the girls could walk in the middle of them or behind them near the fence. They chose to walk in the middle, which led them to an open patch where the boys played football, many barefoot, with a football made of assorted materials. The spectators, always men, sat on the floor, their feet sandy and cracked. As soon as the girls came into view, the men watching the game turned to look at the girls, and one of them said something, and they all burst out laughing.

'Have you come to play, girls?' asked one, who was tall and skinny. The girls ignored him, but he put his hand crudely on his crotch, 'Come and play with just me then. One of you will do; give me the tall one.'

Amina usually called herself 'an after reflector.' If someone insulted her, she would remain silent instead of hurling back insults. She'd dwell on what was said, think of a reply much later and say, 'I wish I'd told him this!'

Now, Amina was outraged. 'Shame on you! And you, an old man! Did your mother bring you up to disrespect women? Have you no sisters?'

In response, he stuck his arm out and made a lewd gesture while the other men laughed even louder.

'Let's go, Amina; he's not worth it,' said Qamar dragging her away but pleased she had been proved right.

What Will Be

Amina had noticed that it was her little sister who had attracted the most attention from the men, and she vowed to keep her close and safe from harm. From that day on, Ayan was stuck like glue to her sister's side. If she went to the makeshift toilet, Amina waited right outside the door; if Anab sent her to fetch water, Amina volunteered to go with her. She had lost her parents; she was not going to lose her sister, the only family she had in the world.

'You're treating her like a baby,' Anab admonished sometimes. 'She can fetch water all by herself; all the other children do it.'

'I just don't want her playing in the dirty water that has collected on the ground. I swear it would be a lake if those wretched children didn't play and bathe in it! Maybe it could be filtered or something, then we wouldn't have a shortage of water.'

Chapter 9

The talk at the camp was almost always about who had found a sponsor or, failing that, who the United Nations had taken out of the camp to faraway places like the United States of America, the United Kingdom or Europe. Camp inmates with relatives abroad were the lucky ones. They got sent money every month, usually dollars, and they played a waiting game. They knew that their relatives would already have told the authorities who and where they were and so were most confident of getting out of the country.

Anab had no relatives, and neither did Amina and Ayan. 'I hope we will not stay here forever,' said Ayan to both of them. 'No, we won't; someone will come for us. I have heard that they take you on the planes even if you have no relatives to sponsor you,' soothed Anab.

'Qamar says she's going to America; she says her uncle lives there. He said it's very nice and safe, and people live in proper houses with indoor toilets and have plenty to eat. The government gives them money even if they don't work.'

'I would take what Qamar says with a pinch of salt,' said Amina. 'She likes to create stories to pass the time.'

'That's good. Perhaps she'll be a famous author one day.'

'Perhaps,' agreed Anab.

'I miss books. I wish I had a proper book to read, not the children's ones that are often distributed around camp, some even in Swahili like we understand the language,' said Amina. 'Remember our library at home, the books...' and her voice trailed off as she fought to forget yet again. Best not remember, she often thought to herself.

The next day Qamar came to the girls' hut with a new announcement. 'Guess what? There's going to be a wedding!'

'What? Who's getting married?' asked Amina.

'You know Suad? Well, she met a man here last year and fell in love. Since she has no one to give her away, our maalim is going to do the honours!'

'When's the wedding?'

What Will Be

'Tomorrow, so get your glad rags ready! Everyone will be there, of course; it's the first wedding we've had since I've been here, so I'm looking forward to it.'

'You are so excited, it's like you're getting married yourself.'

'I will get married one day, but not in this dump. I'll get married in America, in a proper hotel, with lots of food and drink, and music, and I will be wearing new clothes, and my uncle will give me away.'

The wedding was the talk of the camp all week until it took place. It gave everyone something to look forward to, something different from the camp's mundane, hopeless, and joyless life. Everyone chipped in, giving whatever they could. Anab lent the bride her only good remaining scarf. Another woman gave her red plastic sandals, yet another produced an old but clean guntino, the Somali outfit favoured for weddings. Unlike a proper Somali wedding, no one, not even the bride, was covered in gold as is the norm. Cheap, plastic bangles dangled from Suad's arms, and her hair had been newly braided by one of her friends. They had searched all over the camp for wild flowers to decorate her hair, but they found nothing as it was too dry for anything to grow. Her groom had on a maacawis, a lovely green and purple one, and a clean, white T-shirt. He was barefoot.

After the maalim had pronounced them man and wife, they retreated to their hut while the people danced and sang outside. A jerry can turned upside down became a makeshift drum, and a woman beat at it with a stick and sang while everyone clapped. She sang traditional songs praising the bride and groom, their relatives and even their ancestors. The refrain was picked up by the other women, and both men and women danced together. 'This would never happen in Somalia,' the maalim said indignantly. 'Men and women dancing together, unheard of! Is the groom going to bring us a white sheet tomorrow morning, so we can see whether his bride was a good, virtuous virgin?' The woman playing the drum turned to him. 'Old man, go home. This is not Somalia; we are in a strange land in strange times. It is a strange time for everyone, and even if we had a new white sheet, which you know for certain we don't, we wouldn't waste it on that. No one cares right now whether she is a virgin or not. Allah has blessed her with a young, good husband who will take care of her. Let her find whatever little happiness she can in this place.' The old man fell silent.

What Will Be

The dancing and singing carried on for most of the night, enjoyed by both young and old. It didn't matter that they weren't dressed for a wedding, that some of them had no shoes, no new clothes, very little food. For a few hours, they forgot all that and had fun. Tomorrow was another day; no one knew what it would bring.

The days at the camp rolled by, uneventful, occasionally disrupted by United Nation's staff and other international do-gooders. The camp residents thought of them as a nuisance; they didn't bring anything new or useful but always arrived with lots of questions and empty smiles.

Not long ago, a famous Hollywood actress had arrived with her entourage. There was hardly any excitement from anyone in the camp except the workers who knew this famous person. Amina, Ayan and their friends didn't care; they couldn't remember the last time they had watched a film. No such luxuries existed in the refugee camp. There wasn't even a television. The actress, blonde and beautiful, was smiling, patting the little kids on the head, and bestowing her megawatt smile on anyone in her vicinity. The press and the UN staff were fawning all over her. 'She's beautiful,' observed Qamar. 'Look at her clothes and her lovely shoes. I'm going to get those when I go to America.'

'Ha ha, how are you going to afford those? You won't have any money,' Amina laughed.

'You'll see, Amina, I'll get them and then I'm going to send you a photo of me wearing them!'

A young man standing by overheard the conversation. 'I'll get you the shoes if you'll marry me,' he said.

Qamar and the other girls burst out laughing. 'Why would I marry you, a penniless refugee, when I can marry a rich American Somali?'

'You don't even have your own hut; I know you share!'

'You're no better than me, you're as penniless as I am, and you'll never, ever, get to America. Those relatives of yours who say they will sponsor are lying. You are not the first, and you certainly won't be the last person to be abandoned. Those relatives have made a life for themselves in a new country; they do not want to be reminded of poor refugee relatives left behind in a camp in Africa! Your best bet would be to marry me; at least then, you'll have a warm body next to you every night!'

What Will Be

Crushed by his harsh words, Qamar wiped a tear from her eye. He had just put into words what she had been thinking all along. She had been at the camp for five years now, and there was never any news of her leaving, only a few hundred dollars sent every few months via the xawala, the Somali money exchange system. Every so often, a relative abroad would go to an office, send money back to Somalia or elsewhere in the currency of the country the relative lived in, and, for a small commission, the equivalent amount would be sent to an office in that country, which would then get in touch with the recipient by phone, word of mouth or letter and ask them to collect the money or appoint someone to collect it for them.

In the camp, all monies came through Hassan, the UN worker. He was an honest man, and they all trusted him not to short-change them.

Yes, she had been deluding herself. Her sorrow turned to fury. 'Shut up, you dog! You don't know what you're talking about. I wouldn't marry you if you were the last man on earth, you filthy bastard!'

Amina consoled her friend. 'It's OK, Qamar, don't worry, you will get to America. These things take time, and that we have in spades. I wouldn't listen to him.'

Still, that evening, Amina wondered if they would ever get out of the camp, or live, grow old, and die here like so many before them.

Qamar, upset and distracted, wandered around the camp after Amina and Ayan had gone home. At least they had Anab to call them in for supper. She had no one, and no one cared whether she ate or not, whether she lived or died. So engrossed was she in her own misery and self-pity, she failed to notice the man walking behind her. As she turned a corner, he grabbed her by the arm and dragged her behind a hut. She started to scream, but he punched her hard in the face, and she could feel the blood pouring from her nose. Qamar was usually fiery, but she made no effort to protect herself, stunned from the unexpected blow.

'Now we'll see who's filthy, you bitch! Insulting me in front of everyone, do you think you're better than me? Well, you're not; you're just another refugee whore.'

Coming back to her senses, she started begging, 'Please, brother, leave me alone. I'm sorry if I hurt your feelings before; please let me go.'

What Will Be

'I'm not your brother, I'm a man who is going to take what he wants, and I want you. You should have agreed to marry me, then this would be halal!'

Qamar was too shaky and frightened to fight him off and prayed to God for help, but God ignored her.

The man threw her to the ground, lifted up her long skirt up and forced himself into her. The pain was excruciating, but before she mercifully passed out, she could see his face, cheeks stretched tightly over a skinny face making him look like a cadaver, his uneven yellow, protruding teeth and oily skin pockmarked by acne.

Just before she lost consciousness, she prayed again to God that she might live to see this man die a horrible death.

When she came to, she was alone, bleeding and lying in the dirt. She got up and went to the only place she knew she would get solace and comfort.

Anab opened the door, took one look at her and knew something horrible had happened. She ushered her in just as Amina and Ayan rushed over to her.

'Qamar, what's wrong?'

Qamar started sobbing so much she could not speak. Anab had guessed what had happened, and she silently took the young girl in her arms and just rocked her. 'Go boil some water, Amina. We have to tend to Qamar first, then I'm sure she'll tell us what's wrong.' She gently undressed the sobbing girl, and when Amina returned with the hot water, she got Qamar to wash away the blood between her legs and gave her a clean baati to wear. She made a cup of sweet tea and insisted that Qamar drink it.

Amina and Ayan fussed around Qamar but were unsure what else they could do to help and exactly what had happened to their friend.

After her sobs subsided, she told them what had happened.

'Do you know who he is?' asked Anab.

She shook her head. 'But I have seen him around the camp and have never spoken to him other than today when he said I should marry him.'

'Well, unfortunately, there's no law here, and since you don't have brothers or any male relatives to avenge you, there's not much we can do,' said Anab sadly.

What Will Be

Amina was indignant. 'But we can't let him get away with it! He has to be punished!'

'No, child, I could tell the elders about this, but it will be of no use. They can reprimand the bastard, but there's very little else that they can do. No, here's what we will do. We will not tell another soul. If this comes out, it'll be no good for Qamar; her reputation will be ruined. Nobody will believe that she didn't lead him on.'

'But that's outrageous; there's got to be a way of punishing him!'

'No, there isn't, think of Qamar. Can she deal with everyone in the camp knowing she was raped? Think of the gossip the whispers, the stares. We have to keep this between us, please girls'

Although she was desperately sorry for her friend, Amina was still upset about Anab's suggestion to stay silent. Why be silent? He did something wrong; the man should be punished. She kept badgering Anab.

'Amina, let me tell you something. Just like you, I would like to see justice done and for that man to be punished. But as I explained, there is no law here. This is not a country with laws and rules, where wrongdoers get punished and sent to jail. We are in a refugee camp; it's dog eat dog here. You don't know this, but people get killed here all the time. The clan war has followed us here. Only last week, a Darood man stabbed a Hawiye man to death. His body was buried quickly, and the Darood man was still walking around freely in the camp. Do you think he would be able to do that if there was a law? Also, you must understand our culture, Amina. Somali men are brought up to expect to marry virgins. Qamar will not get a husband once everyone knows she's been raped. Do you want that for your friend?'

'No, of course, I don't.' The conversation ended, but the sense of injustice would not end for Amina.

As the days passed, Qamar, once bubbly and lively, withdrew into herself. She never ventured outside the hut despite being lured out by Amina, Anab and Ayan. She helped Anab with cooking and other household chores, but she mostly sat on a stool just by the hut door to watch people without being observed. Whenever she could, she washed over and over again as if to wash away the memory of her ordeal. She often cried silently, blaming herself and asking a thousand questions. 'Why didn't I scream louder? Why didn't I fight back? Was it all my fault? Why did I speak to him in the first place? Why didn't I just ignore him like the other girls did? Who will want me now? I'm soiled goods.' She carried on torturing herself, and once, while chopping onions, she held the knife a little too long in her hand, contemplating cutting her wrist and putting an end to it all. No more dreams of America, of the little house with a garden that she would have, of a husband, of children, of the beautiful shoes she would buy. She could just end it all now. Nobody would miss her.

Anab, wise to the ways of the world, always kept a close eye on her and instinctively knew what Qamar was contemplating. 'This suffering will pass, my child. You will see. You must be strong and survive. A better life awaits you.' Casually, she asked Qamar, 'do you know that suicide is a sin in our religion? The Quran says only Allah can take the life he gave you. Those who take their own lives will surely go to hell.'

'It's OK, auntie, I know and thank you for everything, and I don't know what I would have done without you.'

'Nonsense,' smiled Anab gently, 'you'd have been OK.'

Amina was another one who was far from OK. The rape of Qamar had affected her more than she thought. She kept on thinking about ways to get even with the rapist. What could she do? How could she hurt him without implicating Qamar? She knew she wasn't strong enough to confront him by herself. Truth be told, she was scared stiff, but the sense of injustice would just not leave her. She kept seeing the man around the camp, still watching football, laughing, living his miserable life as though he hadn't ruined anyone else's. 'Qamar, we have to do something. Seriously, I can't sleep or eat, and I can see you can't either. I know Anab says to forget it, but it's easy for her to say that, she wasn't raped.'

'You're right, Amina; we must do something. Only then can we get on with our lives. You might be shocked, but I have so much hatred for him that only his death will satisfy me.'

'I'm not shocked, far from it. I want the same thing as you, but if he is to die, how are we going to do it?'

'Anab also said not to tell anyone, but I've been thinking of telling someone.'

'Who?'

What Will Be

'Remember Burhan from dugsi? I practically grew up with him, we came to the camp at the same time, and he's the nearest thing to a brother I have. If he knows what happened, he might do something.'

'OK, let's go talk to him.'

They walked the short distance to Burhan's hut and called out to him. Burhan, a tall, lanky boy with a big afro, greeted the two girls. 'Do you want to come in?'

'No, we're going for a walk; come keep us company.'

They walked to the farthest end of the camp where Qamar said, 'Burhan, you've been like a brother to me. I'm about to tell you something awful, but before I do that, you have to promise me you will not tell a living soul.'

'What, tell me, you know you can tell me anything?'

'First promise.'

'OK, I promise, now spill.'

So, she did but was not prepared for his reaction. He put his hands on his head and cried. 'Who did this to you, who?'

'Please stop, Burhan. Crying is not going to help me. I've already cried enough for everyone. We don't know his name, but he's one of the men who watch the football.'

'There's a game this evening. Let's go, and you can point him out to me. I'll kill the bastard!'

'That's exactly what I want, but don't go all guns blazing, Burhan, we have to think about how and when to do it.'

Come the evening, they went to the makeshift pitch, and Qamar pointed him out.

'Skinny bastard, I could take him now and beat the shit out of him!'

Burhan was a fearless orphan who grew up in the streets of Mogadishu. 'Let me at him. By the time I'm finished with him, he'll be crying for his mummy!'

'You can't, he's got all his friends with him, and they'd all go for you; let's sleep on it tonight and meet up tomorrow.'

Qamar, Amina, and Burhan had very little sleep that night, each one of them thinking up ways to kill the rapist. They met again after lunch and pitched their ideas to each other. 'I say cut his throat,' said Qamar viciously. What do you think, Amina?'

'I say shoot him like the swine he is.'

'Only one problem,' Burhan pointed out. 'Where are we going to get a gun from? We have no money to buy one even if we could get one. And cut his throat? How are we going to do that? We can't just march into his hut in the middle of the night and do it. I can get hold of a knife, but it'll be a difficult thing to do.'

'OK then, you tell us your brilliant idea, if you have one.'

'I'm still working on it. Give me some time.' Burhan said.

That idea came to fruition two weeks later when he told them exactly what the plan was. He said he couldn't do it alone and needed the girls' help. On the agreed evening the girls went to the football match. They purposely walked past the spectators, and the rapist gave a lecherous smile when he saw them.

'Evening, ladies. Want some fun?'

Feeling sick inside, the two friends smiled at him and, simpleton that he was, he thought his luck was in. Maybe this time, he would try the other one; she had given him an extra sweet smile.

He got up and followed them. As they picked up the pace and walked away quickly, he did the same until he caught up with them.

'I knew you liked it,' he said to Qamar, who smiled falsely albeit broadly even as her heart twisted with murderous hatred.

The sun was setting, and the camp inhabitants were either indoors or heading that way for dinner or evening prayers.

They walked to the farthest edge of the camp, away from the huts and close to the fence that cut them off from the outside world.

The rapist became even more excited. 'I see you two want to be alone with me; you'll have to decide who goes first.'

Up to this point, the girls hadn't spoken a single word to him, and now Amina gestured to him to follow them behind some dry, yellowing bushes. He followed and began to unfasten his macaawis in anticipation.

What Will Be

Amina lay on the hard ground, heart-thumping, she was beginning to think she was mad to have agreed to this, but it was too late now.

'When I finish with your friend, it'll be your turn, so don't be jealous,' he said to Qamar as he knelt, then climbed on top of Amina.

She thought she was going to throw up; his breath stank, not to mention his unwashed body. As he lifted her skirt up, he felt something rough go round his neck, and he put his hands up to his throat to try and free himself. He heard a male voice say, 'Die, you son of a whore!'

Burhan pulled the rope tighter and tighter round the struggling man's thin neck. Amina had quickly escaped from under him and now stood with Qamar; not sure what to do, she just stood there and watched. It was an awful sight, seeing someone fighting for their life.

Qamar moved closer to his face, his eyes bulging now, the tongue purple and protruding, but pleading with her to help. She spat in his face and shouted. 'Tighter, Burhan, tighter!' He squeezed the rope tighter still round the man's neck; really, he could just as easily have snapped his neck and broken it; it was that skinny.

The raspy breathing, as he gagged for air, the jerking of the arms and the kicking of the legs soon stopped.

Burhan checked that he had stopped breathing then rolled the body behind the bushes, out of sight. He knew no one was going to miss or worry about another dead refugee.

'Oh my God! What have we done, what have we done, are we going to be punished for this?' Amina asked hysterically. Apart from her parents, this was the only dead body she'd ever seen. Even though she was the instigator, Amina felt terrible and couldn't share with Qamar's joy.

'No, we're not; he was a bad man who got what he deserved. Don't forget he was going to do the same to you if he had the opportunity. We've done it, we've punished him, he's dead, and now we need to keep our mouths shut and tell no one about this. We still have to live here, so let's forget tonight ever happened; this is a secret that should die with the three of us.'

'Oh, thank you, Burhan, you have proven to be my real brother. I, for one, am very happy and will sleep like a baby tonight,' said Qamar.

What Will Be

The three now shared a terrible bond and the vow never to talk about or tell anyone about what happened that night. A few days later, the decomposing body was discovered by one of the camp inhabitants who walked around the camp for exercise. No-one knew who the corpse belonged to; no-one had missed him as people came and went all the time. If someone wasn't seen for a while, everyone just assumed they'd left the camp and gone abroad to join their relatives.

Chapter 10

Not long after this horrific incident, Qamar's relative in America did come through. She bid a tearful goodbye to Burhan, Anab, Amina and Ayan, who had been like family to her. 'I will never forget you, all of you, and Amina, I will send you that photo I promised you.' She was being sent to Nairobi so that the United Nations could then transfer her to the United States to join her relatives.

After Qamar's departure, Amina became more unsettled and frightened. What if she or her sister were raped? Who would defend them? Who would look after them? True, Anab was there, but she was getting old. What if she died, like Farah? Then it would be just the two of them, with no one to protect them. She had to find a way out of this camp. Otherwise, something awful was going to happen to them.

She did her research discretely. She began by asking people about Nairobi, Kenya's capital. The best person to ask was Hassan, he had long worked for the United Nations, and everyone knew him as the camp coordinator. Although he was Somali, he was born in Kenya, in Wajir, a town in what used to be called NFD, the Northern Frontier District, so named by the British during colonial times. He spoke fluent Kiswahili as well as Somali and was well-liked and respected in the camp. He felt an affiliation with the refugees; after all, they were his people, Somali people. Even though he was born in Kenya, the Kenyans hadn't accepted him or all the other Somalis who called Kenya home and had never set eyes on Somalia. To the Kenyans, he wasn't a mwananchi, a citizen; he was simply waryahey, a term used by Somali men when addressing each other. In Somali, it meant man, but the word had come to symbolise every person of Somali origin in Kenya. The Kenyan Somali had attained a reputation for being fierce, and no one in their right mind would pick a fight with them. Everyone knew Waryaheys carried daggers and were not afraid to use them. Being called Waryahey suited the Somalis just fine; they were, after all, warriors and proud of it.

She walked up to Hassan's makeshift office, and he smiled as he saw her. He recognised her, just as he did many of the refugees who regularly came to ask various questions or just came for a chat to while away the hours.

'Hello,' he greeted her.

What Will Be

'Brother Hassan, I need some information.'

'Fire away, sister, that's why I'm here!'

'Can you tell me about Nairobi?'

'Sure, what do you want to know? And why the interest in Nairobi? Have you got family there?'

'No, I have no family anywhere. It's only my sister and me. But I keep hearing of Nairobi and people going there, so I would like to know about it. Have you been?'

'Several times, our head office is based there. Well, let me see what I can tell you about Nairobi, or Nairobbery as we call it. It's a big city, modern, beautiful, with parks and greenery, lots of people of all nationalities, big shopping malls, and lots of traffic, always busy. It is also the only city in the world that boasts a national park in the city.'

'It sounds lovely, Hassan.'

He laughed. 'Not all of it is lovely. Granted, some areas are beautiful, with huge houses and gardens, but they mostly belong to white people. The Africans live in slums; one called Kibera is the biggest slum in Africa. It's where the poorest live.'

'But where do the Somali people live? I have heard there are lots of them in Nairobi.'

'Oh yeah, they live in another slum that used to be populated by Asians, Eastleigh.'

'I have heard of Eastleigh, some of the people who have left the camp have gone to Eastleigh, and I've also been told that the local Somalis have been very welcoming to us refugees.'

'Yes, we are good that way; we cannot let a fellow Somali suffer and just stand by idly. Almost all Somali families in Kenya have at least one refugee living with them; it is not uncommon to see entire families cramped into a two bedroomed house with the original occupants. Sometimes we are not even related; we just take them in based on clanship or just being Somali.'

Amina pondered this fact. 'So, a Kenyan Somali will take any refugee just because they are Somali? It won't matter what clan I belong to?'

'No, it won't matter. I, too, have a couple and their daughter in my own house, and I don't even know what clan they are. I don't think it's fair or important to ask. Anyway, why all these questions? Do you want to go to Nairobi?'

'I might, but how would I get there? I have no money, and I don't know anyone in Nairobi.'

Hassan looked at the earnest, questioning girl in front of him. Could he help her himself? He had just told her how helpful local Somalis were. 'You live with Anab, don't you? With your sister?'

'Yes.'

'How would they feel if you left them?'

'I won't be leaving my sister. We have to stay together, always. We can never be separated; she's all the family I have.'

'Where are your parents?'

'They were killed in Somalia,' Amina said sadly.

'Sorry to hear that. Listen, I will try and help you get to Nairobi if that's what you really want. But strictly speaking, you are not allowed to leave the camp until either someone claims you or the United Nations takes you out of the country, or you abscond. However, I have seen many people left languishing in here for years, and I wouldn't want that for you and your sister. You are young; you need to live your lives away from here. Leave it with me; I'll see what I can do.'

Amina thanked him and, excited, went to find Ayan. She found her plaiting her hair under the shade of the acacia tree. 'Ayan, guess what? We might be able to get out of here soon. I've just been talking to Hassan, and he said he would help us get to Nairobi.'

'But I don't want to go to Nairobi. I want to stay here with Anab.'

'Well, you can't. I'm older than you, and you have to do as I say, and if I say we're going, we're going, and that's the end of it.'

'But who are we going to live with?'

'Don't worry about that. Hassan will sort it.' Looking at her younger sister's crestfallen face, she changed her tone and spoke to her gently. 'It will be alright. We've gone through a lot and we have survived. We'll survive in Nairobi too. If we don't take this chance, we will stay here forever. Do you want to live here forever? Look what happened to Qamar, it could happen to us too, and no one will do anything about it. And, Ayan, I definitely don't want to die here or live here till I become an old lady.'

What Will Be

'But what about Anab?'

Amina knew Ayan had formed an incredibly close bond with her. Her sister always attached herself to whoever took an interest in her, and Amina knew she was badly affected by Qamar's departure. 'We will ask her to come with us.'

That evening, as they ate their meal of rice and beans, Amina broached the subject of Nairobi with Anab. She explained what Hassan had said to her and added that if it worked and he was really going to help, she would like her to go with them. She had been a good, kind mother to them, and they wouldn't want to leave without her.

Anab was touched that the girls really thought of her as a mother. 'I will talk to Hassan myself to make sure he takes you to a good home. Not all the local Somalis are good, despite what he told you, Amina. I love you two as my own, but I will not be coming with you.'

At this, Ayan started crying, and Anab soothed her.

'There, there, there's no need to cry. I am old, and you don't want to burden yourselves with an old woman. I want you to leave this place too; it is no place for young ladies like you. I will be alright here.'

They both hugged Anab, and Amina said, 'I will send for you one day when we are settled, I promise.'

'Insha'Allah, child. What will be will be.'

Hassan was questioned the next morning by Anab. 'Did you put the idea of Nairobi in my girl's head, you rascal?'

'No, Auntie, I did not. She came up with it; all I said was that I would try and help her, that's all. I didn't make any promises.'

'Well, you can make promises to me, and I will bless you. Promise me you will get them out of here. Promise me you will take them somewhere good. Promise me you will not harm them.'

'Of course, I will not harm them, auntie. I am a respectable family man, and as you can see, I hold a respectable and responsible job. I shouldn't actually be helping, I'm supposed to be impartial, and I could lose my job. But I saw how sad and depressed she was about being here. I have sisters her age, and I can't imagine one of them being in her position. I would have liked someone to help her.'

'How soon can you get them out of here?'

What Will Be

'I have to go to Nairobi on business in the next few days, so I will make inquiries then and see what we come up with.'

A couple of weeks later, Hassan went to see Anab. He never usually went into the refugee huts; they always came to see him in his office.

'Come in and have some tea, Hassan,' she invited him in.

'No thanks, Auntie, I've just had a cup.'

'Well, what news then?'

'Good news, auntie. I've found a home for the girls. I spoke to a man who is well known and well respected in the community. His name is Mohamed, and he has children of his own, ten of them. When I told him about the girls, that they were orphans with no known family, he was very sad and sympathetic to their plight. He said he would look after them and that two more additions to his family would not make any difference.'

'That is wonderful news. I had heard that such kind people existed, but I had never believed it until now.'

'Believe it, Auntie, they do exist. This man has helped several refugees, is well-off and has even paid the airfares for some of them to go abroad. The girls couldn't be going to a better home.'

'When can they go, and how? I've told you we have no money.'

'It's all taken care of, Auntie. Mohamed gave me money for bus fares, food, and anything else. When they go depends on you. You tell me when. He has asked me to phone him when they're ready. He said he would get his wife and driver to collect the girls from the bus station in Nairobi and take them home. I told him about you too, and he said you were welcome too.'

'May Allah heap blessings on him, but as I said, I will stay put. I will be happy knowing the girls will have a future. Let me enjoy them a few more days, then I will tell them the good news.'

'But Auntie, this has to stay secret, just between the two of us. As it is, I have to find a way of slipping them out of the camp and to the bus station without anyone noticing.'

'Don't worry, my son, my lips are sealed.'

Over the next few days, Anab started gathering what little they had into a plastic basket without telling the girls the reason. She insisted that they both wash and fold their clothes neatly and put them in the sisal basket. She

What Will Be

kept herself busy and didn't want to dwell on the fact that she would soon be all alone again. After dinner that night, she told the girls the good news. Ayan immediately burst into tears, but Amina was secretly excited. Nairobi, at last!

Anab comforted Ayan as much as she could. 'Don't cry, my dear. You are going to a better place; count yourself lucky.'

'But I want you to come with us. Please come with us,' she begged.

Anab was adamant. 'You go first, make a place for us, then I will come Insha'Allah.'

It was decided that they leave on a Monday afternoon when the camp was quiet. After lunch, most of the inhabitants went to sleep as there was nothing else to do. It was the best time to head out of the camp and disappear. Some of the refugees, fed up with waiting for handouts from the government or relatives, took matters into their own hands. They walked out of the camp and found other ways of looking after themselves. Often, this meant sponging off a local Somali family or finding poorly paid menial jobs. Few were as lucky as the two sisters, who now had a home and a new family ready to welcome them.

On Sunday night, Ayan instructed Amina to take the basket to Hassan to not raise suspicion on Monday afternoon. On Monday morning, she had a last breakfast with the girls and spent what little time they had together with them. Her heart was breaking, but she put on a brave face for them. 'I will say my goodbye here. After lunch, go to Hassan's office; he will be waiting for you.'

At precisely one o'clock, Amina and Ayan, both in tears, hugged Anab and kissed her goodbye.

'I will send for you, I promise,' said Amina.

'Yes, yes, now go, quickly! Go with my blessings.'

They both looked back tearfully to take a last glance at Anab, who stood in the doorway, her shawl covering her mouth to stop her silent sobs.

It was the hottest part of the day. The thin cotton baati they were wearing did not help. Sweat pouring off them and, in cheap flip-flops donated by someone, they ran into Hassan's office. He was waiting for them and handed Amina their basket.

'OK, let's go,' he said as he led them out of the camp.

What Will Be

They walked in the heat for about ten minutes before they came to what must be the town. Two rows of shops, that was it. Never having ventured out of the camp before, Amina hadn't realised that the town was so close. She could have got there herself if only she had known. Hassan led them to a bus stop, with only one green bus stationed there.

'This is the bus to Nairobi,' he said. 'I've already bought your tickets, here Amina, you look after them. Inside your basket, you will find food and water for the journey. It's a long journey, about eight hours. I've also written down Uncle Mohamed's number for you, just in case, and mine also.'

Amina always wondered why all grown-grown-ups must be auntie or uncle even though they were not your relatives.

'Don't be afraid. I'll also talk to the driver for you.' He found the driver, pointed the two girls out and said something in Kiswahili to him. Amina noticed that he had also slipped some money to him. The driver looked at them, nodded and went about loading luggage on the bus.

The bus did not have many passengers and was due to depart soon. Hassan found them seats at the front, next to the driver. 'I've got to go back to the office now, girls. You'll be safe, don't worry. Look after each other, and I will ring Uncle Mohamed tonight to find out if you have arrived safely. I have to do that anyway. Otherwise, Anab will kill me!'

Amina remembered just in time to say thank you to Hassan. If it wasn't for him, they would still be stuck in the camp. 'We owe you a lot,' she told him, to which he good-naturedly laughed off.

'You don't owe me anything. Go and enjoy your new life.'

During the journey, Ayan wouldn't stop questioning her older sister. 'Will they like us, do you think, the new family? What if they don't? Will they send us back to the camp? Can Anab come to see us? Will we be able to go back see her?'

'Ayan, stop asking me all these questions. What will be, will be. How am I supposed to know whether the family will like us or not? Why wouldn't they like us? We're nice girls. But maybe they won't like you because you moan too much!' Seeing her younger sister's worried face, she said gently, 'Stop worrying. Hassan did say Uncle Mohamed is one of the nicest people in the world. He's agreed to welcome us, complete strangers, into his home, Ayan, don't forget that. A good man is bound to have a good family. Anyway, think of it as an adventure. Nairobi is a big city like Mogadishu....'

What Will Be

She trailed off as she blocked the Somali capital from her brain. They never spoke of it or their previous lives. It was as if it never happened, and they had always been in the camp.

Chapter 11

Nairobi

As the bus neared Nairobi, the scenery changed. The dry, sandy landscape they had been viewing for the last seven hours gave way to a lush, greener one. They could see lots of trees, bushes, and parks. In his rear-view mirror, the driver observed them, their young faces pressed to the window. 'Karibu, welcome to Nairobi,' he said, 'the Green City in the sun!'

When they arrived at the bus station, he told them to wait until all the other passengers had disembarked. The girls watched as everyone rushed off the bus. The bus station was very busy, crowded, and noisy. People were holding up boiled eggs, corn on the cob, pastries, and sweets for sale. They were glad they weren't getting off just yet; they would surely have got lost in the crowd. A little while later, the driver came to get them. He took them to a man holding a board with their names displayed. 'Here they are,' he said to the man and left them.

'I am Kamau, Bwana Mohamed's driver. Mama is waiting in the car. Come with me.'

They followed him as he led them expertly through the throng of people to a white Peugeot 504. Inside was Mohamed's wife, Khadija.

Kamau opened the door for them and told them to get in.

'Hello Amina, hello Ayan, welcome to Nairobi. You must be tired after your journey.'

They shyly returned her greeting.

'Here, have some water, and I also have some sandwiches for you; you must be hungry after your long journey.' Mohamed's wife was a short, beautiful woman with a kind face. They felt comfortable with her immediately as they sipped their water and ate their sandwiches.

The girls couldn't believe how busy the city was, so much traffic, so many people, all rushing off in different directions. They stared in awe at the skyscrapers in the city.

Kamau drove along Uhuru Highway, and they caught a glimpse of the golf course on the right; they had never seen one before and thought it was a carefully tended garden.

What Will Be

'Are we going to Eastleigh, Auntie?' Amina asked.

'No, we are going to South C. That's where we live, not Eastleigh.'

'But I thought all Somalis live in Eastleigh, Auntie.'

'Not all,' corrected Mohamed's wife, Khadija. 'We live all over the city, although Eastleigh is still considered as Little Mogadishu by the Kenyans.'

When they got to South C, the driver stopped outside a big villa and hooted. The iron gates were opened by the uniformed askari who was permanently stationed in a little kiosk beside the gate. The house itself was built in the style of a Spanish villa; it almost resembled their house in Mogadishu. It was a double-storey and painted a bright white.

'Come in, girls,' Khadija said. 'The children are all at school, but the cook will have prepared lunch for us.'

They entered a huge sitting room. For an instant, Amina and Ayan were transported back to their old home in Mogadishu. The house had a familiarity about it; it was as big and opulent as theirs had been. Although tinged with sadness at the memory, they felt instantly at home.

Khadija called out to one of the maids and asked her to show the girls their room to freshen up before lunch. They followed the maid upstairs, walking along a long corridor until she stopped outside a door, opened it, and gestured for them to enter. The maid, a young girl in a uniform and a matching headscarf, spoke only Kiswahili which they didn't speak. They wondered how they would ever communicate with her.

The room was a lovely shade of pink with two single beds and an ensuite bathroom. On the beds were two new baatis, two toiletry bags filled to the brim with all kinds of things and two fluffy white towels. After the squalor of the hut in the camp, this was sheer luxury. After years of washing and bathing from a tin bucket in a roofless bathroom, even having a bathroom again was an unimaginable luxury.

They put their basket on the floor, and Ayan rushed to the bathroom shouting, 'Me first!'

'OK, go ahead, but only this time. Remember, the older one always goes first!' Amina said, laughing.

After Ayan came out, all clean and shiny, Amina went in, stripped, and stood under the hot shower. It was bliss, and she closed her eyes as she soaped herself and used shampoo on her hair for the first time since Moga-

What Will Be

dishu. When she put the conditioner on her hair, she was ecstatic. Her long hair, always knotted at camp, fell to her shoulders, smooth and tangle-free. She was in the shower for so long that Ayan had to shout at her to get out. Auntie Khadija would be wondering where they'd got to. She reluctantly came out of the shower and applied deodorant and Vaseline body lotion and a spritz of the Somali perfume from her toiletry bag. She felt human again, like a girl again, born again.

Both clean and dressed in the new baatis, they found their way downstairs.

Khadija looked at the girls and smiled. They were very pretty, both of them. They had a glow about them now that the dust and dirt of the camp had been washed off them. 'Come sit and eat,' she said as they timidly sat at the dining table. Again, it was reminiscent of a long-forgotten home.

The table was laden with different types of food and drink, as well as freshly made juices. They wolfed down the food as Khadija quietly observed them. Poor things had been starved of good food at camp, she knew. She had seen some of the others who had passed through her house, all skin and bone, but with love and nourishment, they would soon change.

'Where did you put your old clothes?' she asked the girls.

'In our basket Auntie. We will wash them later.'

'No, you don't have to do that. I want you to throw them away, along with the basket. I will give you everything you need. You are members of my family now, and you will be treated as such. Besides, we have maids that do the washing and ironing, so you don't have to.'

'Thank you, Auntie. May the blessing of Allah fall upon you.'

Khadija smiled at that. She knew the girls had been looked after by an old lady in the camp. They must have picked up her way of speaking too. 'You can go rest now. My children will all start coming back from school at five. Then you won't have a minutes' peace!'

Gratefully, they went back upstairs to their room. They couldn't believe their good fortune.

'Amina, we haven't met Uncle yet. Do you think he will be as nice as Auntie?'

What Will Be

'Of course, he will. He is the reason we are here, remember? I can't wait to meet him!' 'Do you think the children will like us?' Ayan asked anxiously.

'I don't know. We'll soon find out. Now do as Auntie asked and get some rest. I'm so full, I feel I could sleep for a week! And this bed, wow, so soft and comfortable. Pour cold water on me if I never wake up!'

By the time they woke up, there was more noise and movement in the house. They went downstairs to the only place they knew so far, the dining room. There, Khadija introduced them to the other children who must just have come back from school. Schoolbags and other paraphernalia dotted the dining room table, laden again with tea, sandwiches, and cakes. Some said hello warmly, some barely looked at the girls, so used to coming home and finding complete strangers in their home.

Only one of the children took issue with the constant comings and goings of strange people in the house. Mohamed's middle daughter Asha always chided her father. 'Dad, why do we always have to have these people here? Can't they go somewhere else?'

He always smiled gently as he answered as she knew he would, 'They have nowhere else to go. It is our duty as Muslims, Somalis and above all, human beings to help them. They have nothing, and you have everything. You must always think about others less fortunate than yourself.'

When he came home from his office that evening, Khadija introduced him to the girls, and they instantly fell in love with him. He was tall and very handsome with wavy hair and a moustache that curled up at the corners. He reminded them of their father.

'This is your home now,' he told them. 'You mustn't act like guests; you're part of the family now, just like my own children.' He questioned them further about their interests, about the camp and about Somalia and their parents. They told him everything about their lives so far and felt even closer to him. They had had a mother, Anab, but they hadn't had a father for so long.

That night, the family all had dinner together as they got to know each other. When Amina and Ayan later went to bed, they slept comfortably and safely for the first time in years. They wouldn't have to worry anymore about food and shelter.

What Will Be

They got up early the next morning, went downstairs and were surprised to see no one up except Khadija and the maids. They didn't realise it was a Saturday, hence, no school, so the children were all asleep. In the camp, every day was the same, you didn't distinguish between weekdays and weekends.

Khadija was surprised to see them up so early. 'What are you doing out of bed so early? Go back to bed.'

'Auntie, we always get up early. We had to help Anab make breakfast every morning.'

'Well, you don't have to do that here, so go back to bed if you want to.'

However, they didn't want to go back to bed, so they stayed and had breakfast with Khadija. They wandered where Uncle was, and she told them he had left early for the office. 'Your uncle works every day. I have tried to get him to have weekends off, but we have him with us some Sundays if we're lucky. You'll see him when he comes home for lunch.'

The household started to wake up from around eleven in the morning. It was a happy, lazy Saturday morning house. The children woke up at different times and had breakfast made to order, each requesting their own favourite. They chatted happily, still in their pyjamas to both girls.

The older girls closest in age to Amina and Ayan informed them that they were taking them out.

Alarmed, Amina asked, 'Out where?'

Ebyan, the oldest, answered. 'Well, since you're new to Nairobi, we thought we'd show you around the city first, then maybe go to the cinema. We usually go every Saturday to the cinema in town or the drive-in near our house.'

Amina and Ayan had never been to the cinema, let alone a drive- in one. They didn't want to appear unsophisticated in front of the other children. Amina smiled as she heard her sister say, 'Oh, we used to go to the cinema in Somalia with our parents all the time.'

Uncle Mohamed came home in the afternoon for the rest of the day, and the car and the driver were both free to use for other family members.

'So, who's doing what today?' Khadija asked the children. Some said they were going swimming, some to see their friends and some, of course, to the cinema.

What Will Be

'Mum, we're taking Amina and Ayan to the cinema,' Ikran informed her mother.

'In that case, you'll need some money. Take this, and give some to Kamau for a drink and some food. I'll tell him to come back after he's dropped you off; I need to run some errands myself.'

'You can't go dressed like that!' Ebyan told the new girls when she saw them wearing their new, colourful baatis. 'You look like you're still in your nighties!'

Embarrassed, Amina replied that they had nothing else to wear, only baatis. Actually, they were wearing the new ones Auntie Khadija had put out for them the night before.

'No, no, come with me to my room, you really can't go out like that. I'll give you something else to wear.'

They trundled upstairs to Ebyan's room, where she proceeded to open a vast built-in wardrobe full of clothes. The girls had never seen so many clothes, so many pairs of shoes since Mogadishu years ago.

Ebyan expertly selected two tops, two pairs of jeans and brought out several pairs of shoes. 'We're roughly the same size, so these should fit you. What size shoes do you wear?'

Having only worn rubber flip flops for all their time in the camp, they had no idea what shoe size they were.

'Don't worry, if my shoes don't fit, you can try my sisters' and if none fit, I'm sure mum will buy you both some. In fact, I'll let her know before we leave.'

When they all came back downstairs, Khadija could barely recognise the new girls. They looked so different, although a little awkward, in what she recognised as her daughter's jeans and t-shirts. They looked like modern young ladies instead of the refugee camp survivors that they were.

'You look lovely girls. It is nice of you to share Ebyan, but I think they need clothes of their own so we can go shopping soon.'

Ebyan gave the girls a glance that said, 'See, I told you my mum would get you something.'

Ebyan, Amal, Amina and Ayan piled into the car and Ebyan spoke in Kiswahili to Kamau telling him what the plan was. He drove them to the city centre, and on the way, Ebyan and Amal pointed out landmarks and places of interest. 'That's Uhuru Park. As you can see, it's full of families on weekends; that circular building is the Kenyatta Conference Centre or KCC as it's known.'

Amina and Ayan took in Nairobi; it really was a beautiful city and so many skyscrapers. Most of the streets were named after Kikuyu heroes, Ebyan informed them. They knew who the Kikuyu were. They had seen some at camp. They were the first non-Somali people they had seen. To them, the names Wayaki Way, Muindu Mbingu Street, Kimathi Street all sounded exotic. On Mama Ngina Street, Kamau parked the car and let the girls out.

Ebyan had decided that they were going to the 20th Century cinema to watch a James Bond film. She bought their tickets, Coca Colas, and popcorn, and led the small group to the cinema's interior, where the usher showed them to their seats. Amina and Ayan sat mesmerised for the next two hours. They watched beautiful women, fast cars, and lovely homes and locations. They were happy for the first time since they'd left Somalia. It was true; their lives had changed and for the better. In their hearts, each offered a blessing for Uncle Mohamed and his wonderful family.

Chapter 12

The girls quickly and easily settled into family life. Ayan was enrolled in the local school, and Amina was enrolled in secretarial college. Uncle said it would give her an edge in the workplace if she learnt typing and shorthand. The car could not take all the children to their various schools, so some were collected by school buses while others used public buses. Amina soon got the hang of boarding the number 13 bus to town and then walking the short distance to her college on Kimathi Street. She is in a class from nine until five, with tea and lunch breaks in between. On her lunch break, she goes out with the other girls from the college between one and two. They usually go to a little cafe and have hot chips and a cold drink.

Her new friends include Maryam, a Pakistani girl from Mombasa and Jacinta, a Kikuyu. This was new for Amina; all her friends had been Somali, the same culture, religion, and language. She found out different things from her new friends. She never knew, for instance, that just like the Somalis, Kikuyus were also circumcised, both men and women. She also found out that Maryam's culture was similar to hers; girls had to be virgins until their wedding day, be respectful and obedient to their families, be pious, and live at home until a suitable husband was found. Jacinta, on the other hand, could pretty much do whatever she wanted. She could go out whenever she liked, she could date, and in fact, she had a little boy out of wedlock that she had left with her mother in the village. As opposed to both Amina and Maryam, Jacinta explained that she was more likely to get married now that she had proved her fertility.

'I wish we were like that,' Amina said to Maryam.

'No, I like our way better; it wouldn't be nice for your husband to find out there's been someone else before him.'

'Don't be ridiculous, Maryam. What about him? Do you think he would not have been with anyone else?'

'But men are different.'

'There's nothing different about them. We all have the same feelings and desires.'

'How would you know? Have you ever had a boyfriend?'

'Of course not. We had no time for such fripperies where I came from.'

What Will Be

'Well then, both of you have to find boyfriends,' Jacinta laughed.

'My brothers would kill me,' said Maryam.

'Why don't we go out one night? There's a nice nightclub that I go to,' suggested Jacinta.

'Oh, I would never be allowed out,' said Maryam. 'I've never even gone to the cinema in broad daylight alone. My brothers always come with me. Haven't you noticed that I am dropped right outside college and picked up straight after? I'm afraid I haven't got the freedom that you have, Jaci.'

'I've never been to a nightclub,' said Amina.

'That's really sad. I wish your lot would move with the times. This is liberal Kenya, now, not Pakistan or Somalia!'

'I know, I know, but you can't just change things that have been in place for centuries. But hopefully, change will come one day. Then we can all have babies out of wedlock like you!'

'I would like to go out one night,' said Amina. 'I will ask my new family if I can and let you know tomorrow, Jaci.'

That night before she asked Auntie Khadija if she could go out, she broached the idea with Ikran.

'Are you mad? You can't tell them you want to go to a nightclub. They'll think you're up to no good. Only loose Somali girls go to nightclubs, according to my parents. But luckily for you, my sisters and I don't think like that. We go to nightclubs, but we don't tell them. We just sneak out of the house.'

Shocked, Amina asked, 'Won't they notice you getting ready, won't they hear when you go out of the house or when you come in?'

'No, silly. We wait until they are asleep. Don't forget this is a big house and our bedrooms are in the west wing. However, we have to bribe the maid and the watchman at the gate. They both love the extra cash. She opens the back door quietly for us to go out, and when we come back, we tap on her window, and she lets us back in. She has a key to let herself in to make breakfast in the morning. The watchman then opens the gate just as quietly for us, and we get into a waiting car driven by one of our friends' brothers. The watchman also keeps the guard dogs away from us, we don't want them jumping up on us. Sometimes they get so excited when we come

What Will Be

back in the early hours that they bark, and that would certainly wake our parents up if they aren't controlled!'

Amina hadn't realised that the girls in the family were so devious; could she be the same? What if the parents found out and kicked them out of the home, sent them back to the camp? Could she take that risk? She wanted to ask Khadija if she could go out one night, but she realised she would have to reluctantly follow Ikran's advice if she ever wanted to go to a nightclub. It was OK for Ikran; even if she was caught, the parents couldn't kick her out of her own home, she was their daughter, but Amina had to be very careful. She wasn't sure a nightclub was worth the risk of being sent back to the camp.

One day after college, Maryam asked Amina to outside wait with her. She explained that her brother would be late and she didn't like waiting alone. Amina agreed, and the girls spent about fifteen minutes chatting and watching the hustle and bustle of Nairobi at the end of the day. People rushed out of offices in droves, some to hurry home, others to meet friends for drinks at the city's many bars. Smartly dressed women walked past, perhaps going on a date or rushing home to a husband and a baby.

Just then, they heard a loud hoot and looked towards the sound. An old black Mercedes pulled up, and Maryam said, 'That's my brother Kamal. He's the nicest of all my brothers. Come and meet him.'

Amina went with her to the car, and Maryam introduced them. When she laid eyes on Kamal, Amina felt a funny feeling in her stomach. He was handsome with dark brown eyes fringed with thick, long lashes, the kind you find on a cow or a horse.

He flashed her a beautiful smile, teeth white and even.

'Pleased to meet you. I must go and get my bus now,' she said.

'Thanks for waiting with Maryam. Come in, I'll give you a lift. Where do you live?'

'No, it's OK; I don't want you to go out of your way.'

'No, bother, hop in.'

On the way, he chatted away but was mainly directing the questions at her. She answered his questions, happy to give him information about herself. Kamal drove on Uhuru Highway towards Jomo Kenyatta International Airport, then turned off the highway, and over the bridge, towards South C, where Amina lived. He dropped her off at her gate, and she said her thanks and byes. 'See you, Amina, I'll give you a lift tomorrow too if you like,' he said.

That night, she could not stop thinking about him. 'What's wrong with me, thinking about a boy I just met! Anab, her camp mother, and Khadija, her adoptive mother, would have a fit if they knew. She remembered Anab telling her to keep away from boys, and here she was, thinking of a Pakistani one!

The next morning and several mornings after, she chose her clothes carefully and applied more makeup than usual.

The girls in the family soon noticed this and teased her mercilessly. 'More makeup! Are you getting married Amina, have you found someone you're not telling us about?'

She ignored them and applied even more make-up. Kamal soon became the only brother who would pick his sister up from college. The other brothers were happy to be relieved of the responsibility. Maryam had also noticed how her brother increased his use of after shave, so strong the car would reek of it. He had also started worrying about his appearance and often asked his sister if he looked good.

Being with Amina all day, she noticed a change in her friend and often glanced at her in class, knowing Amina would not see her; she was daydreaming. A couple of times, Mrs Kariuki, the bookkeeping teacher, would get her out of her reverie by saying loudly,' I think we are boring Miss Amina today!'

Maryam had guessed Amina was in love, and she was delighted; she loved her best friend and wanted her brother to love her too. She would find a way to get them together.

'Let's go see the new James Bond film on Saturday afternoon. My treat,' she told Amina.

'Where's it showing?'

'Odeon.'

'OK, see you there on Saturday.'

Amina had stopped eating and was losing a lot of weight; food was the last thing on her mind. It was now occupied by Kamal. Whenever Khadija

What Will Be

called her to the dinner table, she would say she had eaten earlier with a friend.

Ayan also noticed her sister's weight loss. That night in their bedroom, she asked her what was wrong. 'Nothing's wrong. I'm just happy.'

'Since when did being happy mean not eating? Please tell me what's wrong? Are you ill?'

Looking at her little sister's anxious face, Amina suddenly felt ashamed. She knew why Ayan was worried, they only had each other, and the poor thing thought she was losing her too. 'Listen, Ayan, I am not ill; there's nothing wrong with me. I'll tell you something, but you must promise not to tell anyone. I met a boy, and I like him, but he's not Somali; he's Pakistani.' She went on to tell her sister all about Kamal, how he always gave her a lift home, how he made her feel special. Ayan was relieved that her sister wasn't ill, but she didn't like her not eating.

'You must eat Amina. Don't forget that there was a time we had nothing to eat when we would wish we had more to eat. Here we have everything, and it's a crime and a sin not to eat. And if you don't eat, I'm telling everyone about your boyfriend!'

Twice shamed, Amina agreed to eat sensibly.

At Maryam's house, the family had just finished dinner. 'Dad, my friend Amina and I want to see this film in town. Can Kamal take me?'

Her father smiled at his only daughter and asked, 'But does Kamal want to see it too?'

Kamal, whose heart quickened at the mention of Amina, said, 'No problem, Dad, I'll take her.'

On Saturday, when Amina arrived at the cinema, Maryam and Kamal waited for her in the foyer. Her heart leapt; she hadn't expected to see him on a Saturday.

'Kamal insisted on coming; in any case, my other brothers were busy; hope you don't mind Amina. You know boys and these Bond films!'

After buying a tub of sweet popcorn, they made their way upstairs to find their seats.

'Let Kamal sit between us; he can hold the tub so we can all share,' suggested Maryam.

What Will Be

They sat down and stood up briefly when the national anthem was played before the film's start. Amina barely heard the words which she had learnt in both English and Kiswahili. She couldn't believe she was sitting so close to him.

Oh God of all creation,

Bless this land and Nation,

Justice be our Shield and Defender,

May we dwell in Unity?

Peace and Liberty

Plenty befall our borders.

James Bond chased cars, women, and villains, but Amina couldn't concentrate on the film. She was far too aware of Kamal and how close he was to her. Every so often, he offered her some popcorn, of which she took a small handful. At some point, Kamal got the courage to put his hand on hers. She stiffened, and he suddenly wasn't sure whether he had done the right thing. As he was about to withdraw, she grabbed his hand and held on tight. Kamal smiled, grew more courageous and put his arm around her. They happily sat like that for the rest of the film. When it ended, and they made their way out, Maryam asked them if they had enjoyed the film.

They both looked at her and laughed guiltily.

'Oh, I get it,' she said, noticing their loved-up faces. 'You didn't watch the film!'

Not wanting the day to end, Kamal suggested they go to Trattoria, a popular Italian restaurant and meeting place for Nairobeans. They walked the short distance to the restaurant, found seats and ordered three cappuccinos and three cakes. Maryam excused herself and went to the toilet.

Amina glanced around the restaurant, hoping that the Somali men who congregated there and lingered for hours over one cup of coffee did not know Mohamed and Khadija. They had a habit of telling on girls. 'By the way, I saw your daughter in town. She was having coffee with an Indian man.'

This casual 'telling' had got many a girl in trouble with their families. But she wasn't alone with him. His sister was there, and he wasn't Indian; he was Pakistani and Muslim, although the difference was negligible to Somalis.

What Will Be

'Can I see you tomorrow?' Kamal asked Amina.

'Yes, OK, when?'

'One o'clock? Then we can go somewhere for lunch.'

Amina told him he couldn't pick her up outside the house; she would have to invent something to get out and meet him at the corner of her road. He said he understood, and the date was set.

When she got back home, she told Khadija that she had a project to do with Maryam and that she would be going to her house and taking the bus there at one o'clock. Khadija agreed, thinking what a hard-working girl Amina was. Amina scarcely slept that night; she was so excited.

Early next morning, she woke up, showered, blow-dried her hair, and spent ages selecting what to wear. She settled on a pair of jeans, a white blouse, and white pumps to go with her white handbag. One o'clock seemed such a long time away. She wished she could tell Khadija where she was going. She didn't like deceiving this lovely woman who had been so kind and loving to her. But she also knew that Khadija wouldn't understand. She was old school, very traditional and believed that the boy you brought home or introduced to the family was the one you would marry. Her daughters all had boyfriends, but they kept this fact a total secret, except amongst themselves. The girls all covered up for each other whenever one of them was on a date.

At one o'clock, she waved goodbye to everyone and slipped out of the house. At the corner, she saw Kamal's old car, and happiness washed over her. Her heart was thumping, both with the excitement of seeing him and the fear of being seen getting into his car.

'Hey gorgeous,' he smiled at her as she got in beside him.

'Where are we going?'

'Just for a drive first, then I'll take you to one of my favourite restaurants for lunch. What music do you like?' he asked her as he fiddled with the cassette player in the car.

'I like this, the Bee Gees; they're great.' She didn't like the Bee Gees who sounded whiny, what with their feminine voices, but if he liked them, she would pretend she did too.

'Yeah, I like them too,' she lied. So, they listened to Bee Gees during the drive, Kamal singing along and occasionally squeezing her hand.

What Will Be

The restaurant was just outside town, and Amina was relieved. Hopefully, they both would not see any members of their respective communities. Kamal ordered fish and chips for both of them, which they picked at. They talked and talked and got to know each other, what books they liked, what films, songs, their hopes, and aspirations. They talked about college, his job, his sister, her sister. After lunch, they took a stroll in the gardens and walked right down to the small stream at the bottom of the garden. They sat down beside the stream, watching the water, and listening to the birds singing in the sunshine. It was all so quiet and peaceful. Just then, Kamal put his arm around her and kissed her. She didn't know what to do, having never kissed a boy before. She thought she would die with happiness and wished they could stay here forever, in each other's arms, just the two of them.

So began the romance between Amina and Kamal. From that day on, they saw each other every day during the week when he took her home and every weekend when she pretended to be studying with his sister.

One Saturday, he said to her, 'Amina, I want us to spend a weekend together. I have a friend who owns a house in Mombasa that he can lend me. Can you get away, make some excuse? We could go next weekend.'

She wanted to spend all her time with him and, of course, was quick to come up with an excuse for the family. That night at dinner, she said to Khadija and Mohamed, 'The College has organised a trip to Mombasa as a treat for us doing so well in our end of term exams. Can I go please? I've never been to Mombasa, and it would be lovely to spend the weekend with my classmates. And it won't cost us anything; the college is paying.' She couldn't believe she could lie so easily and momentarily felt ashamed of herself.

'In that case,' Mohamed smiled, 'We can't object. Go and enjoy the coast.'

Amina told Kamal it was all systems go and spent the rest of the week packing and unpacking what she had packed again and again until she was satisfied with the clothes she had. She packed a bright red kikoi to wrap over her swimsuit. No way was she going in a swimsuit without a cover-up; she was shy and had never even put on a swimsuit, ever. She had only borrowed one because she had heard that people swim in the ocean in Mombasa. 'I'll take the bus to college tomorrow,' she said on Friday, preparing everyone for it.

'But Kamau can take you in the morning,' said Khadija.

'No, it's fine, I'll take the bus, and my case is only small, I can manage. Let Kamau drive the others to their activities.' She had agreed that Kamal would pick her up at the usual corner at the end of the road, and on Saturday morning, she waved goodbye and left the house.

Kamal spotted her and came out of the car, took her case, and quickly put it in the boot, while she just as quickly got into the car. She ducked when she thought she saw Khadija's friend on the other side of the road.

They were on Mombasa Road a few minutes later, which was already filling up with the lorries bound for the port and cars with families heading to the coast for the weekend. Amina noticed Kamal turning off and heading towards the airport. 'Where are you going? You said we would stay on this highway all the way to Mombasa.'

'No, baby, we're not driving. We're going by plane. Driving would have taken us seven or eight hours. There is the train, but that would have been overnight. As we only have the weekend, I didn't want to waste our time travelling, so I bought us two tickets on Kenya Airways. This way, our journey is only fifty minutes, and my friend's house in Nyali is not too far away.'

'But I don't have a passport, Kamal.'

He laughed, 'You don't need one, and we're not going abroad, only to another city in the same country.'

'What about your car?'

'Oh, I'm going to park it at the airport for the weekend, ready for when we return on Sunday night.'

Amina couldn't believe she was actually going on a plane. With her boyfriend, to a city she'd only recently heard of.

Kamal parked the car in the designated slot at the airport, and they walked into the domestic departures' terminal. He checked them both in, after which they then went through to departures to wait for their flight to be called. While they waited, she looked around at the waiting room, fascinated by the other travellers. Some were sharp-suited businessmen, a mix of European, African, and Asian. There was the Indian family who were

What Will Be

already munching on the samosas and pakoras they had brought with them from home, a group of young white tourists who looked filthy, some with dreadlocks and all with an assortment of strange but colourful attire. Their sandals showed dirty feet and toenails. Yuck, she thought, as she turned away and her gaze fell on the old mzungu with a very pretty, young African girl.

Kamal saw her looking, and he explained, 'She's a prostitute, and he's taking her away for a dirty weekend. Most of these old white guys can get a young African girl very easily, no matter what they look like. The girls believe that they are all rich, coming from Europe or America. Probably told his wife and kids that he has business in Mombasa!'

Amina tried not to laugh as she asked him, 'Are we on a dirty weekend?'

'Not like that old boy! First, I'm only two years older than you, and second, I love you, and third, I don't have a wife and kids!'

Their flight was called, and the passengers started walking towards the plane. Suddenly Amina broke into a cold sweat. She stood rooted to the spot, unable to move. 'Come on, or the plane will go without us.'

'I'm scared; I've never been on a plane before.'

He took her by the hand. 'Don't worry, it'll be fine, baby. And I'll be sitting right here beside you, holding your hand. Come on, let's go.'

She allowed him to lead her into the plane, where he helped her with her seatbelt and asked the stewardess to bring her a glass of water.

As the plane took off, Amina's stomach lurched. 'I'm going to be sick,' she said, horrified. Kamal would think her an ignorant peasant.

'It's OK, here use this,' he said kindly as he passed her a sick bag. She felt better afterwards and sucked on the boiled sweet the stewardess had passed round once the flight was in the air. Throughout, she clung to Kamal's hand and only let go when they landed at Moi International Airport an hour later.

Chapter 13

Mombasa, Kenya

When the doors of the plane were opened, the heat almost robbed her of breath. She had heard that Mombasa was hot, someone had told her it was the same heat as in Mogadishu, but she never imagined it would be so stifling.

Outside the terminal, Kamal hailed a taxi and gave directions to his friend's house.

She enjoyed seeing the palm trees, the smell of the ocean and closed her eyes, sighing happily.

Kamal watched her, smiling. 'I knew you'd love Mombasa, my darling.'

A short drive later, they arrived at the house. The taxi driver hooted, and the black gate swung open as he drove in.

A man in uniform came running towards them. 'Karibu Bwana, welcome, I'm Juma, the housekeeper; boss told me you were coming today,' he beamed. 'Please come this way; I will show you to your room, then you can please come down for something to eat. Your luggage will be brought immediately to your room by the house girl.'

The house, a four-storey imposing mansion painted a dazzling off-white, seemed to welcome them too. In the shape of Africa, a swimming pool glittered in the afternoon sun, the garden picturesque, with jacaranda trees, hibiscus and bougainvillaea of different colours, pinks, blues yellows, purples, and reds.

Juma took them to the second floor, stopped outside a vast Lamu style door, opened it, and motioned for them to go in. He then left quietly.

Amina, suddenly very shy, looked at the huge bed that occupied the middle of the room. She had never been alone in a room with a man before, and even though she loved Kamal, she started panicking at the thought of just the two of them in a room. Memories from the refugee camp came flooding back, and she swore she could hear Anab, her camp mother, telling her, 'Save yourself for your husband. Don't be spoiled goods. No Somali man will marry a girl who is not a virgin.' Her friend Qamar's rape also forced itself back into her thoughts.

What Will Be

Seeing her distress, Kamal rushed to her side and took her in his arms. Their cultures were pretty similar, and he understood what a big thing it was that she had done for him just by being here. He loved her even more for that.

'It's OK, darling, we're not doing anything wrong, and we don't have to do anything you don't want. Let's go see what the housekeeper has for us to eat.'

Juma had laid out platters of sliced melon, pineapple and mangoes, samosas, fairy cakes, and sandwiches at a table by the pool. He had also brought a pitcher of ice-cold passionfruit juice.

It was almost six o'clock, the sun would be setting soon, and Juma wanted to get away and go to his own quarters. 'What would you like for dinner?' he asked Kamal.

'Uh, nothing, thanks. This will be fine. You can leave us.'

'OK, Bwana, I'll be back tomorrow morning to make breakfast. Have a good evening.'

'Do you think he thinks we're married?' Amina asked Kamal.

'I don't know. Anyway, it doesn't matter what he thinks; he's just here to serve us, but, er, would you like us to be?'

She didn't know how to respond to that and quickly grabbed her drink, but her heart was thumping wildly.

Had he guessed that she fantasised about being his wife, having two children, a boy, and a girl whose names she'd already picked? Insha'Allah, it will happen, she said to herself, but what will be will be. To Kamal, she simply replied, 'Mmm, I'm not sure you're the right one for me.'

He looked at her, baffled for a moment, then saw her smiling and realised she was teasing him. 'Who's the right one for you then?'

'I was thinking Tom Cruise.'

'What! That shorty!'

'But he's so handsome.'

'He's still short!' Tom Cruise held their attention as the discussion went from his looks to his films for a while.

What Will Be

Just as the sun set, the garden and pool lights came on, and everything was bathed in a golden glow. It was magical, Amina thought as they ate their supper.

'The pool looks inviting. Shall we swim?' Kamal asked.

'Oh no, here comes the moment when he sees me in my swimsuit!' she thought. 'Will the water be cold? I don't like cold water.'

'No, it'll be warm; the sun has been heating it all day.'

They went upstairs to their room, and while Kamal changed into his swimming shorts in the bathroom, Amina went downstairs and changed, in the pool house. She tied her kikoi around her waist and, feeling self-conscious, went to stand beside the pool.

'Wow, you look great!' he said to her as he expertly dived in. 'Oh, it's lovely and warm, like bathwater, come on in.'

She dropped her kikoi and put a foot in the shallow end of the pool; she hadn't been in a pool since Somalia, and she hadn't worn a revealing swimsuit either.

Kamal swam up to her, and she quickly got into the water. 'Race you,' he said and sped away. She didn't want to race him; she just wanted to enjoy the water and being with him. On her back now, she could see the stars and smell the jasmine in the garden. She was just so happy and in love.

After the swim, they showered and changed. He was taking her out to the hotel next door, which had a discotheque. She had never been to one before, but she had heard her college mates talking about them, especially Jacinta, who went every weekend.

They walked among palm trees to the hotel. The discotheque was beautiful inside, the seating plum red and inviting, with loud music and flashing multi-the coloured lights. It was almost empty; Kamal explained it was because they had come too early and that by midnight, it would be heaving.

He found a booth for them to sit at and ordered drinks, orange juice for her and Coca Cola for himself. They sat where they were for ages, just talking and occasionally dancing. Amina confessed that she only knew how to do Somali dances, which she learned at camp, so he showed her a few simple moves. Soon, she was swaying and enjoying the music, especially the slow dance when he held her close and occasionally kissed her.

What Will Be

The discotheque had started filling up with Mombasa youngsters, and it got louder and louder. Amina, who was not used to all this, felt the beginnings of a headache, and Kamal suggested they leave. He ordered a taxi at reception, and she asked why, as the house was so close. 'It's late, baby, and although Mombasa is safer than Nairobi, people do not walk late at night. And I don't want to take a risk with you.'

She hadn't thought of that; she just assumed she was safe with him. The rickety old taxi dropped them off at the house, and the askari opened the gate to let them in. They went up to their room, where Amina immediately took another shower and put her nightie on in the bathroom. 'All those people in the disco dancing so close to you. I needed that shower just to feel clean and fresh.'

Kamal laughed and said maybe he ought to shower too as he didn't want her to think him dirty. When he came out of the shower, Amina was still standing by the bed, unsure what to do. What would he think if he found her already in bed? Too forward, badly brought up? He walked over to the bed, flung the covers off and got in. 'I'll sleep on this side, come on, don't be afraid.'

She slipped in beside him, and he turned to her. 'We don't have to do anything, darling. I know you're scared; I'm a bit scared too, to be honest.'

She moved closer to him, and he just held her for the longest time. She felt strange things she could not understand, and when he started kissing her, she did not want him to stop.

'We can just kiss and cuddle,' he told her, but much to her shame, her body was already responding to him. He was intoxicating, this close, and even as Anab's voice came to her again, she thought it was the right thing to give her virginity to this man she loved.

Afterwards, he held her closer still and told her he loved her again and again. She got up to take her third shower of the day, but she only washed the blood away this time, not shame or guilt.

She had heard that it was painful the first time, but she hadn't felt any pain, only pleasure and happiness tinged slightly with guilt. She knew she shouldn't have sex before marriage; both her religion and culture didn't allow that, but Kamal had assured her it was the right thing to do because they loved each other, they would get married anyway, and she believed him.

What Will Be

Nairobi

The weekend flew past too quickly. Amina and Kamal were wrapped up in each other, and soon it was time to go back to Nairobi and reality. When he dropped her off at the usual place near her house, he told her he had a friend who lived close by and that they could use his house for their secret meetings. Amina asked which house, and when he told her, she knew exactly which house it was because she passed it every day on her way to college. With a place to rendezvous, they had no hesitation in beginning their illicit love affair.

They would set their date every time he dropped her off with Maryam, and she began spending blissful weekend afternoons with Kamal. He would bring a takeaway which they would share, and then go to the bedroom for the rest of the afternoon. 'What about your friend? Where is he when we're at his house?'

'Oh, he never stays in Nairobi; he's always away doing something. Camping in Naivasha, safari in Masai Mara or deep-sea fishing in Malindi.'

'Hmm…lucky man.'

'Would you like to go to these places, Amina? I'll take you, but you have to come up with another college trip!' he laughed. Devious Amina did, and true to his word, Kamal took her to new game lodges and hotels where he always checked them in as Mr and Mrs. She went on hot air balloons and on dawn safaris where she saw what the Kenya Tourist Board called the Big 5 – the lion, the elephant, the buffalo, the rhino, and the leopard.

Amina was floating so firmly on cloud nine that she didn't notice she hadn't had a period that month. It wasn't until she started feeling sick in the mornings and couldn't stomach her favourite black forest cake that she suspected something was wrong.

The next time she saw Kamal, she told him how she was feeling, and he went a sickly grey colour.

'Kamal, are you alright? You don't look well,' she asked him with great concern.

'I think we have a problem, baby. I think you could be pregnant.' It was her turn to turn puce. How did he know? But, of course, he was a man of the world; he knew more about these things than she did.

What Will Be

'But I can't be. You told me I couldn't get pregnant because you used condoms. I can't be; it'll be the end of my life, the shame, oh God, and my new family will kill me, or at best disown me. What will then happen to my sister and me?' She sobbed violently as Kamal tried to comfort her. 'Look, let's be sure first. We're getting ahead of ourselves here. I will make an appointment for you with a doctor to find out for sure. And if it's positive, we will get married, so don't worry.'

However, he was deeply worried and panicking though he tried not to show Amina his fears. He remembered shifting a bit and slipping the condom off in Mombasa. It would be his fault if she was pregnant.

That night, she couldn't sleep and kept tossing and turning, sobbing soundlessly so Ayan couldn't hear her. Shame, guilt, and nausea washed over her all at once. Why, oh, why did she sleep with him in the first place? Was God punishing her for committing a sin? Please God, let me not be pregnant, she prayed. I promise to be good, and I will never go near Kamal again. But she also told herself he had said he would marry her, which was a good thing. Insha'Allah, everything will be OK. What will be, will be, but please, please God, don't make me pregnant, she prayed fervently.

Chapter 14

The next day at college, Maryam rushed up to Amina. 'How was the weekend? Did you have a good time?' She knew her brother and her best friend were in love and inseparable, and she was happy for them. 'Whoa, Amina, those are serious eye bags you're carrying, sister! What were you doing last night? I know Kamal didn't spend the night at your house!'

Great big teardrops rolled down Amina's face, and Maryam's teasing turned instantly into concern. 'What's the matter? I was only joking about the eye bags.'

'Oh Maryam, the most awful thing. I missed my period last month, and we think I might be pregnant.'

Maryam gasped in shock. She hadn't realised that her friend had gone all the way with her brother. What a stupid girl! Everyone knew not to do that, you could kiss and touch, but you couldn't ever go the whole way unless you were married. 'What are you going to do?'

'I don't know, but Kamal is taking me to a doctor this evening when he comes to pick you up. Please come with me; I'm so scared.'

'Of course, I'll come with you, silly.'

When they got to the doctor's, Kamal told the girls to take a seat, walked up to reception, and said something to the fat woman sitting behind the desk. She glanced at the two girls, nodded, and Amina felt her face burning with shame. 'We're a bit early, so we'll just wait.'

There was another couple in the waiting room, the woman proudly displaying a huge tummy, and the husband occasionally looking up from his paper and patting his wife's hand. They look so happy, Amina thought. And here I am, scared out of my wits. The couple were asked to go through to the doctor by the receptionist and, after about fifteen minutes, came out smiling, hand in hand. Then it was Amina and Kamal's turn.

The doctor was a kindly old Indian, but he raised his eyes slightly at the couple. It was unusual seeing a Pakistani and Somali couple, although they looked too young to be married. But you never know these days, he thought; he saw more and more unusually matched couples. 'What can I do for you today?' he asked, and Kamal explained. 'OK, go behind the screen and take your pants off.'

What Will Be

Amina, panicked, clung to Maryam's hand. 'Come with me.' Maryam went with her and watched as her friend slowly removed her jeans and was standing just in her knickers.

'You need to take those off,' Maryam said.

'But why?'

'How else is he going to examine you, silly?'

She had never been examined by a doctor before, and he was a male doctor, and she was about to expose her most private part to him. 'I can't do this, Maryam, how embarrassing that he can look at me. Couldn't your brother find a female doctor?'

'Don't be stupid, Amina. He's a gynaecologist; he spends his days looking at women's bits!'

Amina giggled nervously at that and took her knickers off. 'I'm ready,' she called out to the doctor, and he came in, told her to get on the bed, and he started examining her. She tensed, both with embarrassment and discomfort, as he examined her.

After a while, he washed his hands, told her to get dressed and left the two girls.

When they came out from behind the screen, he said, 'Congratulations to both of you. Your wife is six weeks pregnant.' He watched, stunned as the wife started sobbing, and the husband shrank back in horror. 'Aah, they are not married,' he twigged. They are in trouble. 'Is everything OK?' he asked. 'Usually, news like this is met with tears of joy, but I can see yours are of sadness.' Because he seemed kind and non-judgemental, they confided in him and told him the truth, which was just as he suspected. 'What will you do now? You can keep it or have a simple procedure to remove it.'

'Well, I'll marry her, of course, but first I have to tell my parents. Amina can't fathom the thought of telling her people,' explained Kamal.

'That would be the best solution, but here's the number of a clinic if you change your mind, but please don't leave it too late.' They thanked the doctor and left.

Kamal dropped Amina off home and prepared to face his parents. After dinner, he broke the news to them and at first, they just stared at him, uncomprehending. His father, who was shorter and smaller than him, pushed

What Will Be

his chair back, went over to his son and slapped him hard on the face. 'Of all my sons, you are the most irresponsible, the most reckless, and the one who hangs out in clubs and chases girls. Why can't you be more like your brothers, good boys who pray and go to mosque? You have ruined not only your life but that of a decent girl!'

Kamal, his cheek stinging from the slap, said, 'But I want to marry her. I love her.'

His mother wailed as his father calmly replied, 'Well, you can't.'

'What, why? Because she is not Pakistani? I don't want a Pakistani girl, I want Amina, and you can't stop me from marrying her!'

'Listen carefully, son, it's not because she isn't Pakistani. It's because you have already got a future wife. When you were little, your auntie Nazia's daughter was promised to you. So, you will have to marry her.'

Kamal stood up enraged, 'When was I going to be told about this, on my wedding day? Besides, Auntie Nazia lives in the UK, and no way am I going there. And I hate her fat, ugly daughters!'

His mother then gave him the second slap of the day. 'You will not talk like that about your cousins. Have some respect. Kulsum can have any man she wants, she's got a good job, and she's a good God-fearing girl.'

'I don't want to marry her; I don't love her.'

'Love has nothing to do with it,' his father said at the same time as Kamal bizarrely thought of Tina Turner singing 'What's love got to do with?' that he'd heard on the radio on his way home. 'That is what happens in Bollywood films, not in real life. This is a matter of honour, family honour.'

'Well, I'm a grown man, and I can do what I want.'

'A grown man? Who still lives with his parents? Who works in my factory? Who drives the car I bought, lives in my house, wears the clothes I buy, eats the food I buy?'

Shamed, Kamal wasn't giving up without a fight. 'You can have the car back, and I'll get another job.'

'Oh yeah, where? By the time we broadcast your shame, no one will want to employ you, let alone know you. I'll make sure of that, you bastard!'

'That's not fair, Dad! You can't do that.'

What Will Be

'Life isn't fair, son, so don't push me into ruining yours. You'll do as you're told for the sake of the family honour and our good name.'

His mother tried a different tactic. 'Islam teaches you to obey your parents and be respectful. It also teaches that you should get married. Your cousin may not be the one you'd choose as a wife, but the deed is done. Don't shame us in front of the whole community by being a disobedient son, and please don't cause a rift between my sister and me. Think of your only sister Maryam; she won't find a husband if you disobey us. Can you live with that?'

She used all her wiles as a mum and a woman to make her son think reluctantly that maybe she was right. She had cried, used emotional blackmail as well as the tried and tested 'I'll kill myself' that she used whenever things were not going her way.

He loved Amina, but his loyalty was to his family; the family honour mattered above all else, even as he was doomed to a life of misery and loneliness with someone he didn't love.

After the family drama, he shed bitter tears in bed that night, not just for himself but for his love Amina. How could he tell her that he couldn't marry although he loved her deeply? How would she take it, and now, in her condition too? He cursed the day he was born into a Pakistani family with its many rules and regulations. He thought about getting Amina and eloping, but how could he do that, with no money, job, or car? He developed a new hatred for his parents. How could they just plan his life like that without giving him a thought? They kept telling him they did it because they loved him, but what kind of love was it that made your child this unhappy?

The mosquitoes buzzed round his head, and he wished one of them would bite and give him malaria so he could die. He could also kill himself, but that was a cardinal sin. For the first in a long time, he wished he didn't have to wake up and face Amina the next day.

In the morning, Maryam went to comfort him. She looked at his miserable face, and her heart went to him.

'What am I going to do, Maryam? How do I give her up? How do I tell her that what we talked about isn't going to happen, especially now?'

'Mum and Dad are unfair, but you know what they're like; in the end, we all do what they want. I'm just as sad for both of you, but you have to tell her today. Remember what the doctor said, if she is going to do something about it, she needs to do it now. Do you want me to come with you when you meet her today?'

'Yes, please, sis, I don't think I can face her on my own.'

Amina was surprised to see Maryam when Kamal picked her up at the usual place. Of the three, Maryam looked the freshest. Amina and Kamal both had dark circles under the eyes, and the unshaven Kamal in his crumpled clothes didn't look appealing at all. He drove them to an old hotel in the outskirts of town. Amina was wondering why Maryam was there; she had never accompanied them on their dates before. Kamal ordered three cappuccinos and broke the news to the stunned Amina. Maryam held her hand as the tears rolled down her face.

'What am I going to do now, Kamal? What about me? Who will want me now? Mohamed and Khadija will kick me out when they find out. Where will my sister and I go? I thought you loved me.'

'With all my heart, Amina.'

'Then why? Why are you agreeing to marry someone else?'

'I'm being forced to, Amina.'

'What do you mean forced? You're a man; you can simply say no!'

'Believe me, I tried to, baby. But you don't know my parents, they are adamant I marry my cousin. It's all about saving face for them, even though I will be miserable all my life.'

'I'm so sorry, Amina,' Maryam said, dabbing away her own tears.

Amina glanced at her, and at that moment, she hated her friend. If it wasn't for her, she wouldn't be in this mess. She wished she'd never met her, never met Kamal.

The elephant in the room reared its head. 'What about the baby?' asked Maryam.

Amina, who had no more tears, said, 'Obviously, I can't keep it now. Kamal, can you ring the clinic and make an appointment for me tomorrow?' From deep within, Amina's sense of self-preservation and survival kicked in. She'd made up her mind not to crumble. She was a strong nineteen-year-old, she had survived a civil war, the murder of her parents and countless other atrocities, and she would survive this. She would get over Kamal and forget him in no time. After all, who wants to marry a weak man? A sheep who is led everywhere by the nose and can't stand up to his parents? No,

What Will Be

she deserved a real man, one who would stand up for her, protect her and defy anyone who told him not to marry her. Besides, her community would never have accepted a Pakistani who they considered inferior. An Arab, yes, they were people of the Book, a Pakistani, never. So perhaps it was for the best that he was marrying his cousin. Maybe God had other plans for her.

'I'll ring now, from the reception,' he said sadly and left. Five minutes later, he was back and told them he had made the appointment for ten o'clock the next day and he would come and get her at nine. She coldly told him not to bother, but he insisted.

They both endured another sleepless night, Kamal wrecked with guilt and sadness, Amina with guilt and worry. The next morning, he came at the agreed time, and they drove in silence to the clinic. There, he paid at reception, and a nurse took them to a room where she gave Amina a hospital gown to change into. Shortly afterwards, a doctor came to see them.

'You are Amina, yes? I will do the operation; it'll be about fifteen minutes. The anaesthetist will be along soon. The nurse will show you to your bed.' Fifteen minutes later, it was over, and just like that, their relationship was over too, the last remaining tie gone. The nurse gave her some painkillers, and sanitary pads to use over the next few days and asked her to come back if the bleeding did not stop.

Kamal's heart ached, that could have been his son or daughter, and the tears flowed freely from his eyes, but Amina didn't care. He tried to hold her hand one last time on the way to her house, but she pulled away. She didn't feel anything, she was numb, and all she wanted to do was get away from him. He stopped at her corner and turned to her. 'Amina, I love you. Please look at me. I'm hurting too.'

'Good,' she said coldly, 'because all this is your fault, and I will never forgive you for this. I hope you can live with yourself.' With that, she got out of the car and slammed the door shut, leaving him without a backward glance with him sobbing in the car as he watched the love of his life walk away.

Chapter 15

In the years that followed, Amina finished college. She got a job as a secretary in a large construction company in town which she enjoyed. Months later, through the grapevine, she had heard that Kamal had got married and gone to live in Leicester. She felt a slight pang, nothing more. How quickly love can turn to hate, she thought.

Maryam had tried to keep in touch with her, but Amina had made it plain that she wasn't interested; she didn't want any reminders of Kamal. She had made new friends and was beginning to enjoy her life again.

She enjoyed her job but hated the boss. He had been put in the post of managing director by his friend who owned the company Amina was working for. Rumours were circulating in the business community that he had been sacked more than once from several prestigious firms for fraudulent behaviour.

He was from Mandera, a small town in northern Kenya. Although he was Somali, he didn't look it; he looked more Luo, another Bantu Kenyan tribe. He was short, fat, and bald with a loud irritating voice.

In the short time he had been in charge of the company, he had amassed a small fortune through corruption and wheeler-dealing. Not to mention putting his relatives, many of them illiterate, in prime positions in the company.

Whenever he was away, the whole office, including his relatives, breathed a sigh of relief, the office a happier place.

His poor secretary, a lovely Kikuyu girl with who Amina was friendly, bore the brunt of his bullying. He was a bullying sociopath who lacked all the social graces. For example, he would bellow from his office for her to bring it in when he wanted tea. Amina was going to another office just past his once when she witnessed one incident. Lucy took tea in for him on a tray, and he suddenly turned on her. 'Where's the honey? Didn't I tell you I don't take sugar anymore? Are you thick or what?' Amina quickly fetched honey from the kitchen and gave it to him.

Lucy was shaking at the vitriol, and Amina spoke to him in Somali and said, 'You've got your honey boss, let the poor girl go.'

'Poor girl, poor girl? She's bloody useless, bloody Kikuyu!'

What Will Be

Amina was so shocked at his outburst she was left speechless.

'Get out of my office, both of you!' he spat.

Amina stared at him; she was mesmerised and didn't move. He had big teeth, yellowed from years of smoking, and was literally foaming at the mouth. As she took Lucy's arm, she couldn't suppress a giggle; he really looked like a mad donkey, teeth barred with his big, wet fat lips flapping open and displaying the black gums. He actually foamed in the mouth like a rabid dog.

She went to the toilet with poor Lucy, who was now sobbing. 'I hate him; if I didn't need this job, I'd have told him where to stick it. But you know I have two kids to look after, as well as my mother.'

'Don't worry about him, Lucy. You know it's not just you; everybody hates him.'

'I know I shouldn't say this, but I pray for him to die every day.'

Amina laughed, 'I'm sure you're not the only one praying for that happy event, but as we say, God doesn't want evil people, so he has to stay here longer. I mean, he smokes, he eats junk, he's diabetic, he's old, he's fat, but he's still here.' She'd been told by his gossipy driver that he never fasted during the holy month of Ramadhan. While the Muslim males in his office went to the mosque on Fridays for prayers, the driver took him to a nearby hotel for a three-course lunch.

'He's also a thief Amina, I've seen him stuff dollars into an envelope and put them in his briefcase.'

'Well, that doesn't surprise me; I heard that if the company needs furniture or stationery, he makes sure it goes to his son's company, you know the one in accounts.'

'Yes, that's true; he actually told me once to order a desk for the office from his son.'

'Corrupt bastard!'

'Oh, and another thing Amina, everyone who does business with this company has to give him his 'cut' or facilitation fee as he calls it. Can you believe that?'

'Oh yes, I can, isn't that the norm in this country? No one will lift a finger for you unless you bribe them.' Apart from the horrible boss, she got on with everyone in the office and slowly recovered from her ordeal and missed Kamal less and less.

Leicester

In Leicester, Kamal was less happy. His nikkah to Kulsum was done in Nairobi at the Jamia mosque. It had been quick and simple signing his life away. The Imam said a few words; the dowry was set at $5000, and, witnessed by his dad and two brothers, Kamal put his name to the certificate tying him forever to his cousin. He had flown to London, and his aunt and uncle came to collect him from the airport and drove him to Leicester. He was cold, even though he was wearing the second-hand winter coat sourced from the local market in Nairobi. He knew it would be cold, but not this cold.

His aunt chatted all the way there while his uncle concentrated on the road for the next two hours. 'It's not cold for us, Kamal, wait till winter proper when it snows. Then you'll really feel it.'

Kamal noted how courteous and orderly the driving was and thought fondly of Nairobi, where there were no driving rules, and everyone was king of the road.

They pulled up outside a little semi, and he was amazed at how similar the houses and streets were. He picked out his aunt and uncle's house instantly. It was decorated with fairy lights of different colours and orange garlands, signifying that a wedding was taking place at this house.

'This is your home now. Come, come,' Auntie Nazia said as she beckoned him in. 'Kulsum is not here; she's spending the night at Uncle Rashid's. It's bad luck for you to see her now. You'll see her tomorrow at your wedding party, which we have arranged at a local community hall.'

That night, he ate very little of the food his aunt prepared for him and excused himself to go to bed on the pretext of jetlag. He missed Amina so much, but he knew she hated him now, and he couldn't blame her.

Maryam had told him of her last meeting with Amina, ranting against weak, indecisive men. She would be equally disgusted now when she discovered that he had been shipped off like a girl to another country. Normally, the bride moves into the groom's house, but here he was, a man, in another house, in another country. All because he was too weak to say no and follow his heart.

What Will Be

The next morning, his aunt gave him his wedding suit to wear and told him to get ready. They had to be at the community hall by one. He would be taken there by male community members, and his bride would join him there.

He dressed in his cream silk Sherwani kurta and black Shalwar but eschewed the elaborate red turban with the huge gold glass brooch. He didn't want to look like a maharaja, and by not wearing the turban he was given, he gained back a little bit of dignity and control.

'Oh, my, how handsome you look,' his aunt sighed when he came downstairs all dressed. 'All my friends will be jealous of me now with my handsome new son-in-law.'

The house started filling up with men, some similarly dressed and some wearing western suits. The photographer who would also record the event dragged his big video camera and his trusted old Minolta.

His uncle said it was time to go at around twelve, and they all filed out of the house. A minibus decorated with glittery ribbons and flowers was waiting at the end of the road for them. One of the men had a drum and starting beating it rhythmically as they walked to the bus, the photographer snapping away.

At the sound of the drums, curtains twitched, then suddenly all the neighbours came out to witness the spectacle. Kamal thought it was like a guard of honour, curious white faces on either side of the road, watching him and his colourful procession walk down the road. God knows what they thought of the interruption and noise in their usually quiet suburban street.

The hall was small but also decorated brightly, and he was taken in by ushers and shown to a chair that looked like a throne. He sat down with his uncle and another man he did not know but assumed was a relative and awaited his bride, not anxiously.

Soon the beating of the drums heralded her arrival, and she was brought in, accompanied by her sisters and mother. She was wearing a beautiful red bridal dress, but he couldn't see her face; it was covered with a gold veil. He could see that she was of average height but plump.

The drumming and singing intensified as she was slowly led to her new husband. She took her place beside him, and as she was his wife officially, he could lift the veil to see her face.

What Will Be

Encouraged by his aunt and now new mother-in-law, he lifted the veil and was pleasantly surprised. Although she was fat, she had a lovely face, hazel eyes, and a clear, radiant complexion. She smiled at him revealing small, uneven white teeth. It could have been worse, he thought.

His friend Shakil was married to an ugly girl with a limp, so he was grateful his cousin looked like she had no disabilities. Sure, Kulsum was fat, but he could help her lose weight.

Relaxed, he smiled at her as she gazed at him, not in the shy way new brides gaze at husbands they'd never met, but in a brazen, knowing hussy type of way which unnerved him a little.

While they studied each other, the guests around them tucked into their food, occasionally looking up and admiring the bride and groom.

After a while, the bride and groom were led out, and everyone stood up to get the last glimpse. A heavily decorated white Mercedes was waiting to transport them to the house, followed closely by another car that carried the other female members of the community.

At the house, they followed the trail of red rose petals that led to the bridal room. 'From now on, this is your room,' his aunt said with pride. 'Now we will leave you two lovebirds alone while we go back to the party. Kulsum, you know where everything is. Look after your husband.'

As soon as they were alone, Kulsum threw off her veil and took off her bridal gear. 'Thank God that's over! I hate Pakistani weddings, all that fuss and fakery for nothing.'

Kamal laughed for the first time in a long while. She had an English accent tinged with a hint of a Pakistani one. 'It was OK; it wasn't that bad.'

Just as he was warming to her, she jumped into bed and said, 'Come on then, let's do it. We're married now, so it's all kosher, or should I say halal!'

He had never known a girl so brazen, but he just thought that the Pakistanis born in the UK were different from those he knew back in Kenya who were so shy they wouldn't dare look him in the eye.

He got into bed with her, and she immediately wrapped her arms around him and kissed him. Wow, she was a great kisser, he thought as he stroked her, and she expertly stroked him back.

She grabbed him, shifted a little and pushed him into her and started moaning. Aroused, he started moving in her, and it was only after, both of them still breathing heavily, that he realised she was not a virgin. He shrank away from her, and she noticed instantly. 'What's the matter? Wasn't I good?'

'That's the trouble; you're too good! How many others have you slept with?'

'Fuck you, you arsehole. That is none of your business. Why are you shocked? You thought I'd sit here waiting for you? For my 'wedding night?' I'm British, man, not some Paki fresh off the boat! Are you a virgin? Did you save yourself for me? No? Well, I didn't either, so live with it! That's why I can't stand Pakistani men; they expect virgins while they go whoring until and after their wedding.'

He wasn't a virgin, but it still shocked him that his wife wasn't. He did not care much anyway, but he felt cheated and wondered what his mother and her mother would say when they found out.

She read his mind. 'Well, when are you going to do the big reveal? Bet you can't wait to tell everyone that your new wife is a whore!'

He put his head in his hands. Is this what he had left Amina for? A shameless excuse of a woman? 'Shut up, I need to think.'

'Don't exhaust your brain cells. Go and tell everyone. I didn't want to get married to you either. I have a boyfriend, and just like you, I was forced into this,' and she burst out crying.

He looked at her, and a wave of pity suddenly washed over him. He was a man, he would get another wife, but if he told on her, she would be ruined and never get married again. Even though she was wicked, she was still his cousin and hadn't they always said blood is thicker than water? 'Don't worry, Kulsum, I won't tell. It'll be our little secret. You're right; who am I to judge?'

She looked at him with new respect; she hadn't expected this at all. 'Thank you, cuz, I won't forget this and I will try and be a good wife to you. And at least you don't have to teach me what to do,' she added mischievously.

He smiled, looked round the gaudy bedroom, and thought, yes, maybe the marriage would work after all.

Chapter 16

Nairobi, Kenya

In Nairobi, Amina received a letter from United Nations High Commissioner for Refugees, UNHCR. They were relocating her and her sister to the United Kingdom. She was to come to their offices to sign papers and be given proper documents. She showed the letter to Mohamed and Khadija, who were happy for the girls. 'Good job we registered you with them when you came to us.'

'But Auntie, we're not happy. We don't want to leave; we love being here with you. This is home for us now.'

'Think of the opportunities for both of you in the UK,' Mohamed advised. 'You could do anything you want, go to university, and get a well-paid job.'

'I have my job here.'

'Yeah, and how much do they pay you a month? It barely covers your expenses. We love having you here too, but I'm telling you what I would tell my own daughters. Get out of here if you can.'

The rest of the family were happy for them too. 'I'm so envious,' said the eldest daughter, Amal. 'I wish I was going to the UK too. You'll forget all about us when you go.'

'You can come to visit,' said Amina. 'And how can I forget you? You're my sister; you're my family.'

Ayan cried for days; she didn't want to go to the UK. 'Amina, let's just stay here, please. Why do we have to leave? Tell them we're staying.'

'Uncle says it's a good chance for us; we're lucky. Lots of people want to go to the UK, but they can't, and we can, legally. Look at it as an adventure, and uncle has said we can always come back here.'

The thought that they could come back made Ayan feel better, she would go with her sister, and once she was working and earning money, she would head straight back for Nairobi. So, she agreed to go with her sister to the UNHCR office, where they were photographed, fingerprinted, and issued with blue United Nations travel documents and plane tickets. They were to leave the country in less than a month.

What Will Be

That allowed Khadija time to buy the girls new suitcases and warm clothes for the UK and for the girls to have their farewell parties with their friends. She would miss them, they were such good girls and had completely settled into her family, but she believed the time had come for them to leave.

All too soon, the departure day loomed, and Mohamed prepared to take the girls to the airport. He watched as his own daughters and wife tearfully hugged the girls and felt a lump in his throat. He would miss them too; he had come to look on them as his own. The driver had loaded the cases in the boot, and the girls sat in the back as the car drove out of the gate and into the street. With tears streaming down their faces, they looked behind and waved at the family, who all stood at the gates to see them off. They waved until the house could be seen no more and carried on weeping.

'Girls, stop that,' Mohamed comforted them. 'Insha'Allah, we will all see each other again, and you know you both have a home and family here. If things don't work out, you can always come back. Plus, you have my phone number, any problems, call me.'

He took them to the designated spot where they were to meet the UNHCR official at the airport. A few other sad-looking youngsters were huddled together, the blue travel documents clearly visible. The youngest was ten, and Mohamed wondered who had abandoned this poor little boy.

'Name?' the official asked. They gave their names, and he ticked them off.

'Excuse me,' Mohamed said. 'May I ask who is accompanying the girls to the UK? I hope they are not going alone; you see, they have never travelled before, not on a plane.'

'None of them have ever been on a plane before Bwana. Don't worry, my colleague over there will go with them all the way to London until they are handed over to the UK authorities. He will take good care of them; as you can see, we have some real minors flying out today.'

Mohamed walked over to the escort and introduced the girls. 'Please look after my girls.'

'We look after everybody,' came the gruff reply, quickly changing to a smile as he saw the bundle of dollars Mohamed had in his hand. On the pretext of shaking hands, Mohamed passed the bundle to the man. 'I will definitely take special care of them now,' he smiled, almost licking his

What Will Be

greedy lips. When converted into Kenya shillings, that bundle would be enough for him to keep his mistress in hair weaves for months. 'OK, you girls, stick with me from now on,' he said as he led them to the check-in counter. 'Come on,' he called to the others in the group, and one by one, they were checked in.

At the departures gate, Amina and Ayan turned to Mohamed and hugged him close, still crying.

'Go, God be with you. Go with my blessings, my daughters. Oh, I nearly forgot, take this Amina, so you have some local currency for when you get there,' and he passed her another bundle of notes, but this time they were Pounds Stirling. She cried harder at this; he was still looking out for them, right to the end. He watched them until they disappeared behind the immigration and customs booths. He turned away sadly and walked back to his car.

Inside the departures lounge, Amina automatically grabbed Ayan's hand. 'Stick close; I don't want to lose you here.'

'There are so many people, where they are all going?' she asked her elder sister.

'Oh, I don't know. All over the world, India, USA, UK, Saudi Arabia, take your pick.' She remembered the last time she was at the airport, but it wasn't this busy, and there had been no duty-free shops in domestic departures. With a slight pang, she thought of Kamal and wondered how he was faring in the UK. Might she bump into him in the street? She hoped not; she had nothing to say to him.

The small group sat together until their flight was called. Kamau, their escort, appeared very efficient and knowledgeable as he navigated his way to the departure gate, waiting lounge and finally on to the plane. He went personally to check that everyone had their seat belts on and asked the purser to help his group with whatever they needed before take-off.

Ayan sat next to her sister, shaking with fright.

The plane was big, with so many people on board, but Amina seemed calm. What would Ayan say if she knew that it wasn't her first time on a plane? She probably wouldn't believe her; she would think she was making up stories just to reassure her. But she was scared too; Mombasa was only fifty minutes; this flight was nine hours. Nine hours! How would they cope? But cope they did, and after a few mishaps and help from a fellow passen-

What Will Be

ger, they had worked out how to watch films on the little screen, how to go to the toilet alone and without fear, how to ask the friendly stewardess for an extra blanket or more water. One time when Amina went to the toilet, she found a queue and patiently waited her turn. Next to her was a Swahili woman from the coast who she struck up a conversation with her. Like most women from that part of the world, where gossiping was a way of life, curiosity got the better of her, and she started asking Amina personal questions.

'Why are you going to the UK? Have you got relatives there? Which city are you going to?' She answered politely that she didn't know and was going there courtesy of the United Nations. 'Lucky you,' the woman said. 'I'm travelling on a Kenya passport, which I'm going to rip up and chuck in the toilet before we land. This way, I am stateless, and they will have to give me asylum. A lot of my relatives have got into the country like that, and now they have British citizenship.'

Amina thought the woman incredibly brave to tear up a passport and put herself at the mercy of the British. She also thought her a bit dim for revealing something like that to a complete stranger. She was glad she didn't have to do that herself, she wouldn't have had the guts, and besides, she always prided herself on her honesty. She wouldn't do anything as underhanded as this woman.

A couple of hours before landing at Heathrow Airport, they were served breakfast, and they tucked into their choice of scrambled eggs, rolls, fruit, and orange juice.

Chapter 17

London, UK

When they landed, Kamau got his charges together and led them into the terminal. The sheer number of arrivals both amazed and frightened Amina and Ayan. She knew from her geography class that the UK was a small island. Where were all these people going? Did they all live on the island?

The queue for non-British nationals was so long, she was sure they'd be there all day. However, Kamau took his group straight to another desk, manned by a UN official and handed over all their travel documents.

The official checked the documents, stamped them, and said, 'Welcome to the UK folks!'

Kamau took them to collect their baggage and led them out. He spotted the man holding high a sign with his name on it at arrivals and went over. 'I believe you're looking for us.'

'Please come this way; the minibus is parked just outside.' The man loaded the luggage into the van and ushered everyone in. He drove out of the airport and into central London.

After another hour in traffic, he pulled up outside a house with the sign B&B highlighted and offloaded both his passengers and their baggage and drove off.

Kamau rang the doorbell, and a large, blonde woman came to the door. 'Come in, come in. You're the group from Africa; we've been expecting you.' They followed her, each dragging their suitcases. She checked them in and assigned rooms for them. 'You stay in today, rest and unpack. I'll come back tomorrow. Anything you need Mrs Smith will get for you, and she will cook your meals too. She has a list of everyone's dietary requirements.

'This will be your home for the next few months, so be good!' Kamau warned. When he left, they all felt abandoned all over again. True, they didn't know him until yesterday, but he was the last link to home and everything familiar.

Amina and Ayan unpacked in the small room allocated to them. It had twin beds, so close together they were almost touching, and a small toilet. The tiniest kettle she had ever seen stood on a corner shelf, with two tea bags, two sachets of coffee, two biscuits, two lumps of sugar and two creamers. 'Let's have some tea,' she said to Ayan, who was looking lost and bewildered. She added water to the kettle, boiling it twice to make a second cup. She handed one mug to Ayan and sipped from the other. The tea was awful, weak, and watery. She added another teabag to her mug, thinking it would taste and look better, but it didn't. It was still a horrible grey-brown colour. She screwed her face in disgust which brought peals of laughter from her sister.

'Oh Amina, you should see your face! Someone would think you were being tortured!'

'I may well have been. This tea is disgusting. I wonder where they get it from? Definitely not 'Out of Africa,' and no hawash, no ginger, no cardamom, oh what I wouldn't give for a proper cup of Somali tea!' Laughing, they stood by the window and watched people going on about their business.

Mrs Smith knocked on their door at six and took them to the tiny dining room where the other refugee children were seated. 'Dinner is at six, prompt,' she told them, and everyone agreed and nodded, too fearful of saying that, in Africa, that's when babies and little kids had their dinner.

The dinner was nothing to write home about, a small piece of white, boiled chicken, a few boiled carrots, and boiled potatoes. Instead of the fresh fruit juices they were used to, they were given a watery orange squash. It was the most tasteless meal the girls had ever eaten.

'I wish we had some basbas or some other chilli sauce to jazz this meal up and make it more palatable,' Amina said to her sister in their language. 'If we carry on eating like this, I might just give up on food, but hopefully, it's just for today because she doesn't know what everyone likes.'

Unfortunately for them, the meals didn't vary or improve, but other things did. Kamau had taken them to the Home Office in Croydon and formally registered the refugee children. Amina was amazed at the sheer number of foreigners at the Home Office; even amongst the staff, she noted the Indian and African faces amid the odd white one.

Ayan said, 'I can't believe we're in England. This is just like being in South C. Look at all those Somali people sitting there.'

Amina looked, and yes, the waiting room was like a veritable United Nations. The Somalis sat huddled together, still in their sandals and summer clothes, some talking loudly and some just staring into space. Shifty lawyers in dark suits hung around and occasionally whispered something to them. Indians in their colourful saris also huddled together, Arabs and Africans in traditional outfits all competed for a place in the United Kingdom. Like Amina and Ayan, some were the lucky ones; they were here legally and could stay. For many others, luck would not be on their side. They would spend months, if not years pleading for asylum, being exploited by lawyers and community groups before getting the coveted Indefinite Leave to Remain, ILR, stamped on their travel documents. The ones who didn't get this precious document would eventually disappear and join the masses of illegal immigrants who lived and worked anonymously in the country, always looking over their shoulders in case they were caught and sent back to their home countries.

After several months with Mrs Smith, Amina and Ayan were given a one bedroomed council flat in Westbourne Grove, a rather nice area of London. Amina had heard that refugees were given the worst houses in the worst areas, so was very happy when they were shown around their new flat. It was perfect for the two of them. The furniture wasn't to her liking, but she could change that. It was just lovely having their own place and not having to share the bathroom or the kitchen.

With the help of a lady from the council, Amina soon found a job. She was lucky because she could speak English and did not have to go first for the dreaded ESOL, English for Speakers of Other Languages. Her secretarial skills from the Nairobi College served her well as she began her first job as a Personal Assistant to the boss of a major bank. Her boss, Mr Green, was a kind, middle-aged man. Although she was initially intimidated, she soon became comfortable and grew to love her job and London. She also enrolled in one of the London universities as a part-time student, studying for a business management and marketing degree.

Ayan, meanwhile, had enrolled in the local college and was also making friends and enjoying her new life. She had met some other Somali girls in college and regularly went to their homes for lunches and dinners. She often returned to the flat carrying containers full of Somali food to share with an appreciative Amina. The more Somali people they met, the less homesick they became and the less they missed Mohamed, Khadija, and the Nairobi family.

What Will Be

On Friday nights, Amina went out with some of the girls from work to the pub near the office. Ayan disapproved of this, telling her big sister, 'We do not go to pubs. We are Muslims.'

'I'm not going to drink alcohol there, Ayan,' she reassured her sister. 'I only have orange juice and, really, I just like the atmosphere, everyone happy and chatty after a hard week's work. Besides, it's a British tradition, and since we are British now, we have to embrace their traditions!'

'You're wrong, Amina. Just because we have a piece of paper saying we're British doesn't make us truly British. And it doesn't mean we have to abandon our culture and our values.'

'I'm not abandoning anything, little sis. I'm proud of my culture and traditions, but that doesn't mean I can't appreciate another culture.'

So, while Amina embraced the western culture, Ayan fought hard against it, which delighted her new Somali friends. They were all refugees but hell-bent on rejecting British culture, which they thought of as un-Islamic. Instead of wearing jeans and T-shirts like all the other students in college, they wore the two-piece burka or extra-long skirts and veils. Soon Ayan ditched her jeans and started dressing like her friends. Amina didn't notice at first because they left home at different times in the morning. By the time she returned from work, Ayan would have changed into a kaftan or her pyjamas. She felt poorly one day, and her boss said she should go home. She hopped on a bus and was soon home. It was bliss having half a day off work, she thought as she changed out of her work clothes and made herself a cup of tea. She settled in front of the T.V. in the small sitting room and watched Jeremy Kyle. She always enjoyed it but couldn't believe that people like those on the show actually existed. Today's topic, 'My mum slept with my boyfriend,' had her gasping in disbelief.

She had a pleasant afternoon, and just before three, she heard the key in the lock, and Ayan let herself in. Amina stared at her in shock. Her sister was covered head to toe in what looked like a black shroud. 'Ayan, what on earth are you wearing?'

'I'm wearing a modest Islamic outfit,' she said stiffly but removed the veil and her cape instantly.

'Why? Since when?'

'Since ages. You just never noticed because you're never here. You're either at work or with your friends in the pub,' she said accusingly.

What Will Be

Amina cursed herself. How could she have let this happen? Why didn't she see it? Whilst she was having fun, her little sister had been influenced by what she called 'the born-again brigade,' people who had never been religious in their own country but suddenly discovered its virtue and turned to it in their host country. She wasn't against this per se, but she didn't want her sister part of it; she felt she was too young and still needed to learn about life. She tried to explain this to her, but Ayan was adamant. This was what she wanted.

'And I'm going to start going to prayer circle on Fridays,' she informed her sister.

'Well, I suppose you're old enough to do what you like and if you want to go around looking like a ninja warrior, who am I to stop you?'

'Maybe you should start dressing like me and come with me to prayer meetings.'

'Don't push your luck, and please don't start preaching. I can't stand preachers!'

From then on, the sisters grew apart and began to lose their special bond. Whereas before, they cooked together and watched television together in the evenings, now each went her separate way. Ayan would go into her room for prayers and spend the night reading the Quran, only coming out occasionally to eat or drink something. She barely glanced at Amina, who would be sitting alone on the sofa, holding her mug of tea tightly to her chest. Whenever she caught a glimpse of anything on the television, she would stop and offer her opinion. 'Look at that girl; she's practically naked; you can see her knickers, shameful. That's why we need Sharia Law in this country!'

'Ayan, this is a Christian country; you cannot have Sharia Law here; please stop saying things like that.'

One Saturday afternoon, Amina came home from food shopping and found Ayan and three of her friends in the flat. She greeted them politely and went into the kitchen to put the shopping away. 'Anyone want anything? Tea, cake?' They declined, and Ayan followed her to the kitchen.

'Amina, I'm leaving.'

Amina turned to her. 'What? What do you mean you're leaving?'

'I'm going to live with Amal and Samira's family.'

What Will Be

'Why Ayan? What don't you have here at home that you think you'll have at their house?'

'They are a decent, practising Muslim family, and I feel at home there. They treat me like one of the family.'

'But what about me? I'm your sister, your only family.'

'But I feel lonely here, even when you're here. You don't need me. You have your own life. These are the sisters I go to mosque with; I like the feeling of belonging to a community, a community that accepts me, thinks and looks like me.'

'We used to laugh at women who dressed the way you are now. Remember, we used to call them ninjas. Now you've become a ninja.'

Ayan retorted, 'I like it. Maybe it's time for you to cover up. You're a Muslim, and Islam says we should cover up.'

Amina had always maintained she'd wear hijab when she wanted to, not when someone told her to. She found Ayan's preaching boring, but because she didn't want to lose her, she said, 'OK. I'll try and go to mosque, study group, whatever with you, but please don't go, Ayan, and I do need you. You're my little sister; it's always been just the two of us. I have no -one else but you, you know that.'

Despite Amina's pleas, Ayan refused to stay and Amina, with tears in her eyes, watched her little sister walk down the stairs and away from her. The small flat suddenly felt huge and empty, and she curled herself on the sofa and wept. She had always had her sister, she couldn't remember a time when they hadn't been together, and now she blamed herself for her departure.

At work the next day, everyone noticed how unhappy she was but in true British style, and not wanting to intrude, no one thought to ask her why, not even the people she considered friends. She plodded through her work, speaking to no one, only the occasional 'yes 'or 'no' whenever she was asked a question relating to work. She stopped going out for lunch with the girls and refused after work invitations to the pub. When she got back to the flat at the end of the day, she didn't cook for herself. She saw no point in cooking for just one person. She rang her sister every day, pleading for her to come back, but Ayan had moved on and refused to come back.

What Will Be

She loved living in a family atmosphere, she told Amina. It reminded her of being at home with Mohamed and Khadija and their children. 'Pray Amina, it will bring you peace,' she often told her sister, but praying was the last thing on Amina's mind.

Like an automaton, she went to work each day and came home and sank deeper into depression and self-pity. Her work started suffering, and Mr Green warned her more than once. He liked her, but he had started to notice little mistakes in her work and that she appeared listless and sometimes unkempt. She seemed very different from the immaculate and beautiful young lady he had hired on the spot. He knew she had refugee status, and some employers did not like to hire refugees. Still, he was of the group that believed in giving everyone a chance. He also knew that, often, refugees and immigrants worked much harder than his own countrymen.

He called her into his office. As she came in, he noticed her dejected and defeated manner. 'Sit down, Amina,' he said kindly.

She sat and looked down, holding back tears. She knew why he had called her in. He wanted to sack her, and that would be the last straw.

'I can see things haven't been easy for you over the past few months. Do you want to tell me what's going on? I might be able to help.'

She breathed a sigh of relief. He wasn't going to sack her after all. 'I'm fine, thanks for your concern, Mr Green. Nothing I can't deal with.' She glanced round the big office; she had been in here so many times but had never sat down in one of the plush black leather seats. Her eyes rested on the antique silver frame that housed a photo of his family. His wife, pretty but overweight, and two red-headed children, a boy and a girl who very much looked like her father. 'I'm fine, really, Mr Green.'

He knew she wasn't truthful, but he didn't want to push her any further. 'Very well, then. But if there's anything I can do, my door is always open.'

'Thank you, Mr Green,' she replied, touched. He really cared, she thought.

Nothing changed after that meeting, and Amina slowly continued to unravel. When she came home from work, there was no one to talk to, laugh with or have dinner with. The nightmares started and continued, night after night. The man struggling for life, eyes bulging, and a noose round his neck became a frequent unwanted visitor. She woke herself up most nights, screaming and covered in sweat. Night after night, she pleaded with him

What Will Be

to go away, but he wouldn't. 'Please, I'm sorry, I shouldn't have sentenced you to death. Please go away, forgive me.' Apart from this man, she saw the armed soldiers shooting at her, making her wake up with a start. She had read somewhere that if you died in your dreams, you really did die, but if you wake up before you're shot, you live a longer life.

In her nightmares, she re-visited Somalia and the camp and was very happy on waking to find that she was in neither place. She came to work with dark circles under her eyes and so exhausted from not eating and not sleeping properly that Mr Green often found her fast asleep, with her head on the desk. She had also become more talkative and spouted gibberish about soldiers and guns.

He finally took action when she came into his office to bring him documents to sign but dropped them on the floor and screamed.

'What's wrong, my dear?'

'There, there,' she gestured wildly behind him, and he looked.

'There's nothing there, Amina.'

'Can't you see? The soldier, he's behind you, he's coming to get me, and he's got the gun.'

'There's no one here but me. Come and sit down dear, have some water.'

He managed to calm her down, but was alarmed and shocked to the core. What had happened to her, to change her from the intelligent, cool, calm, and collected person he knew to this shivering, gibberish wreck? He rang HR to inquire about her next of kin; the girl was clearly troubled. They gave him Ayan's number, and he rang her immediately. He quickly found out she was the younger sister who did not live with Amina as he had assumed. He told her what was happening, and she said she had noticed changes in her sister and that she was planning to move back in to help her with whatever she was going through. Mr Green told her he would give Amina a month of paid compassionate leave effective immediately and could she come and collect her.

When she got to the office, Ayan too was shocked at the state her sister was in. She was still sitting in Mr Green's office, her eyes vacant and her fingers ripping a tissue into pieces. 'Amina, I'm here; I'm going to take you home.'

What Will Be

'I think she needs to see a doctor,' Mr Green said, and Ayan said she would make an appointment for her as soon as possible.

Suddenly Amina snapped out of her reverie. 'Ayan, what are you doing here? Shouldn't you be in college?'

'It's OK, Amina. I asked her to come and take you home. You need to rest.'

'But I'm fine, Mr Green, honestly, just a little tired. If you'll both excuse me, I've got to get back to work.'

'You can come back to work when you're rested, but for now, you need to go with your sister. I'll order a taxi to take you home. Good luck Amina, and Ayan; please keep me posted, and let me know if there's anything, anything at all, that I can do.'

Amina was reluctant to leave, but Ayan took her by the hand like a child and led her away from the office.

When they got home, Ayan made her sister some soup and gently coerced her to eat it. Then she put her in the bed and told her to sleep.

'Stay with me,' Amina said, and Ayan's heart melted. This was her sister, who had always been there for her and had always looked after her. She had been a mother, and father rolled into one for her. How had she abandoned her? She got into bed with her and held her close.

'I'm here now, and I will never leave you. Go to sleep now.' The roles were reversed, instead of Amina always looking out for Ayan, it was now Ayan's turn, and she rose to the occasion.

While Amina slept, Ayan made an appointment with the doctor, cleaned the flat thoroughly and cooked. She also rang Amal and Samira and told them she was not coming back to the house tonight or for the foreseeable future. She explained in brief about Amina and told them she had to look after her sister now. She didn't get much sleep that night. Amina tossed and turned, often waking up screaming, and Ayan simply held her and calmed her down. She was seriously worried about her sister and couldn't wait to get to the doctor in the morning.

In the morning, Amina didn't want to go to the doctor. 'I'm fine; I don't need to see him.'

'Too late, Amina, the appointment's already been made, and we're not cancelling.'

What Will Be

In the waiting room at the doctor's, anyone could see Amina was troubled. She was quiet, but her eyes kept darting nervously around, once again tearing her tissue to shreds, and Ayan had to keep picking them off the floor. When her name was called, she followed Ayan to the doctor's office.

Dr Patel was a skinny, old man who had lived in the UK for several years. He had first met the girls when they had registered at the surgery. Being from East Africa himself, he had struck up an affinity with both of them and often practised his long-forgotten smattering of Kiswahili with them. 'Jambo, my dears, what seems to be the problem?' Although he had lived in the country for many years, he still had not lost his Indian accent.

Ayan told him about her sister while he listened intently. He then turned to Amina and softly started asking her questions. At the end of it, he said he thought she was suffering from some kind of stress and that he was going to refer her to the psychiatric unit immediately. He said it normally took six weeks to be seen, but he would call in some favours to ensure she was seen urgently. He rang while they were in his office, and within five minutes, he had secured an emergency appointment for them. 'All done, take this letter together with my notes for the psychiatrist with you and go now to the hospital. They will let me know her progress. Good luck, Amina.'

They hopped on the bus again, for the second time that day. At the entrance to the psychiatric unit, Amina stalled again, refusing to go in. 'Ayan, this is a unit for mad people. I'm not mad. What is wrong with that stupid Patel? I'm not going in there; let's go home.' Deep down, she was terrified, she knew she was not right, but sometimes, albeit for brief periods, she felt like her old self. At the doctor's, she had felt disorientated. Now however, here, in front of this miserable grey concrete block, she felt like herself and couldn't understand how on earth she was standing here to see a psychiatrist. And Ayan shouldn't be here with her; she should be in college, going to her lectures and gossiping with her friends. Just then, she saw him, the soldier with the gun. He was grinning at her, his front teeth chipped and blackened. 'Ayan, let's go, even he doesn't want me to go there.'

Alarmed, Ayan asked who she was talking about. 'The soldier, he's coming towards us, can't you see him?'

'I can't see anyone, Amina. Please let's just go in.'

'But, he's coming, he's coming!'

What Will Be

Ayan, though frightened, decided that the only way to get her sister to go into the building was to play along with her. 'Oh, yes, I see him, but if we go in now, he can't come in with us, he won't be allowed to. So, let's go in quickly before he sees us.'

'Ok, let's go, quick, quick!'

At the reception, Ayan gave her sister's details and was told to wait for a few moments. She looked around the waiting room and saw four other people. Some behaved like Amina, throwing furtive looks but others just sat silently staring into space. All of them were accompanied by either a social worker or some other person in a uniform. Soon after, it was their turn to be called in.

The psychiatrist was a young man and seemed very friendly. He greeted them and gently asked Amina some more questions. His were different to Dr Patel's. He wanted to know where they had come from, when they had come to the UK and many other personal questions. He kept apologising too. 'Sorry, but I have to ask these questions.' Was there a history of mental illness in the family?

'No.'

He asked Amina whether she had ever had suicidal thoughts, and she responded, 'Never. It is against my religion.' Did she have support other than from her sister? Did she have friends, community support? Did she hear voices? Amina replied in the affirmative. 'Dr Patel's notes tell me you have recurring nightmares. Tell me about these. I think they may be related to what happened in Somalia. Can you tell me what happened?'

After intense and thorough questioning, he said he thought she was suffering from Post-Traumatic Stress Disorder, PTSD.

'What's that?'

'I was just about to explain that. It is a mental condition that's triggered by a terrifying event such as what you witnessed as a child.'

'Am I going mad, Doctor?' Amina asked.

'Oh no, you mustn't think that. You are not going mad. This is treatable, don't worry. It's a common condition; I've seen and treated many patients from Somalia and other war-torn countries. I want to see you again and work with you through this difficult time. Over the next few weeks, I would like to try trauma-focused cognitive behavioural therapy, but first,

What Will Be

I'm going to prescribe you sleeping tablets for a short time, so at least you can get some sleep. Your condition is not helped by a lack of sleep. I will also prescribe some medication to relieve the secondary symptoms of your anxiety.'

Both sisters were relieved they had a name for what was happening to Amina. Now that it had been explained by the psychiatrist, they both felt happier and better able to cope. Ayan was worried her sister would be sectioned and spend months at the psychiatric hospital. However, the psychiatrist had assured her that Amina's condition could be managed at home.

That night they slept fitfully, and the next morning, Amina even woke up hungry and was able to eat scrambled eggs on toast.

Mr Green, unfortunately, could not keep Amina's job open for the months it would take for her to complete her therapy and reluctantly let her go. However, he wished her well and asked that she keep in touch, and when she was better, he would help her find another position. Ayan took her to the mosque where the Imam read the Quran over her. Special verses were read to ward off whatever evil ailed this unhappy girl. Ayan then did her best to look after her sister, ensuring Amina ate and slept enough and took her medication.

Chapter 18

The months passed, and Amina attended her weekly therapy sessions without fail. She had put on a bit more weight since her appetite returned but nothing that a few gym sessions wouldn't get rid of. Now that she wasn't working, she spent her time in the gym; her therapist said the exercise was good for her and should be considered part of her treatment...

Today, she had done a spin class, a tough one led by one of the professional trainers at the gym. As she showered, she laughed to herself, remembering one of her friends saying, 'I can't believe we have to pay to sweat in the UK while we sweated buckets for free in Africa. We sweated just by standing outside!'

She felt good; she was sleeping throughout the night, the soldier with the gun and the strangled man becoming a distant memory, pushed to the recesses of her mind.

Amina finally confessed to her part in the murder in therapy, still maintaining that her sense of injustice made her do it. The therapist was the only other person who knew her secret, the secret she had put so far to the back of her mind it was as if the murder had never happened. Apart from exercising and eating well, she had enrolled on a second-degree course because she had the time now.

She dressed and, on a whim because she had nothing better to do, decided to go shopping on Oxford Street. Ayan had been a God send; she decided she would get her a present for all that she had done for her. She went into Selfridges, she loved this shop but now that she had no job, found she could not afford anything there, so went out again to try her luck at one of the cheaper shops. Oxford Street, as was customary, was crowded. She jostled for space with the throng of tourists and locals who came here daily looking for bargains. She saw the Africans, the Indians, the Arabs, the Chinese, and other people whose heritage she could not distinguish, all hauling large shopping baskets and bags.

Someone brushed past her, and she clutched her handbag closer to her. She didn't want pickpockets taking what little she had. And then her heart stopped. Coming towards her was someone who looked like Kamal. As he walked past her, he stopped and stared at her in shock, then turned back towards her, his eyes and hers not believing what they were seeing. In that

What Will Be

crowded street, in central London, was Amina. She turned to look back too, and they slowly walked towards each other.

'Amina, is it really you?' he asked.

'Is it really you, Kamal?'

'Oh my God, it is you! What are you doing here, Amina? It's been years, I never ever thought I'd see you again'. People pushed past them, some impatiently, but they just stood there, looking at each other, each thinking how surreal this was, them meeting here after all this time. In the end, Kamal said, 'We can't just stand here in the middle of the road. Let's go somewhere we can talk. Let's go to McDonald's over there.'

They made their way to McDonald's, where he ordered two lattes while she found a booth for them to sit. He came back with the coffee, and they sat opposite each other, studying each other. 'You haven't changed at all, you're as beautiful as ever', he said to her.

'You have, what's with the beard?' He had grown a big bushy beard; he had also put on weight making him look shorter and older than he really was. He didn't look like the tall, slim, handsome boy she had fallen in love with in Nairobi. She told him how she had ended up in London but left out the part about her mental health problems. He didn't need to know this about her. 'What about you? How's your wife? Do you have kids?' At the mention of his wife, she saw tears in his eyes and immediately thought that maybe she had died. 'Oh Kamal, I'm sorry, what happened?'

'Oh, she's not dead, far from it. It's just that I wish I'd never married her. I didn't realise she was the town bicycle; everyone rode her. She wasn't even a virgin on our wedding night; someone had been there before her husband.'

She thought him hypocritical but said sympathetically, 'I'm so sorry, Kamal. I thought you were happily married and living in London.'

'Wrong on both counts. Actually, I don't live in London, I live in Leicester. I'm here visiting a friend. What about you, are you married?'

'No, I haven't found Mr Right yet.'

He surprised her by saying he hoped she hadn't. That's when she realised how selfish he was, how selfish he had always been, but she hadn't seen it when she had been blinded by love.

'What, you don't want me to be happy?'

What Will Be

'I do, Amina, but I don't know if I could bear the thought of you with someone else. I always thought it would be you and me. I haven't stopped thinking about you all these years.'

'Well, there is no you and me, and there never will be. You made your choice Kamal.'

'That's where you're wrong, I didn't make it, and it was made for me.'

'Even worse. I cannot respect a man who can't make his own choices.'

'I want you, Amina. I can't let you get out of my life again. I've been so miserable all these years, tied to a woman I don't love while the love of my life is sitting here opposite me.'

She stared at him coldly, relieved to feel nothing like love for him. She had fantasised about meeting him for so long, and in her fantasy, he would be telling her exactly what he was telling her now. Yet, at this moment, face to face with him, she didn't really want to hear anything he said. 'You should have thought of that when you made me get rid of our baby and left me to marry your cousin.'

'Please don't be so hard, try and understand the position I was in; my mum threatened suicide for God's sake!'

'But she's alive and well, isn't she?'

'Yes....'

But Amina had had enough. She had felt happy today for the first time in ages, and here he was trying to bring her down with his problems. This had nothing to do with her; he had brought it all on himself, he had made his bed, and now he must lie on it. She stood up and looked at him with pity and without love, one last time. She couldn't believe that she once loved him so much. 'Look, Kamal, I'm sorry you're not happy, but there's nothing I can do about that. I must go, thanks for the coffee and take care of yourself. It was good to see you. Goodbye.' And with that, she walked out of McDonald's, leaving Kamal and his misery behind.

He watched her leave with tears in his eyes, not even noticing the strange looks he was getting from the other customers. She wasn't the miserable little girl he had abandoned in Nairobi; she was a woman now, stronger, and more confident. He may have thought of her all these years, but it seemed that she had scarcely given him a thought; he only popped into her mind occasionally when she had her 'what if 'moments. He was in her past, she

What Will Be

had her future ahead of her, and she would live it and live it well. Her therapy was nearly at an end, and she vowed to get a better job and lead a full productive life.

Leicester, UK

After the meeting with Amina, Kamal returned home to Leicester with a heavy heart. His aunt and wife soon noticed that he wasn't his usual self; he seemed even more detached from them. Out of respect for his aunt and uncle, he at least used to conduct a civil conversation with his wife, but now he barely looked at her or talked to her. Not that she cared, but her mother did. 'You have to find out what is eating your husband. How are you going to give me a grandson if you don't even talk?'

'That's his problem, innit Mum, I never wanted him to marry me, and he was your choice, not mine. And if he doesn't want to speak to me, great! I don't want to speak to him either!'

'Don't talk like that, you silly girl. Find out what's wrong, and pronto!'

Kulsum was grateful that he spared her shame, that he hadn't left her immediately he had known she wasn't a virgin. Any other Pakistani man would, but her cousin was kind and decent, at least give him that. But she couldn't love him; she still loved her boyfriend, who had also since married, also under pressure from his family. They still saw each other, though, and the only thing that kept her happy while she was married to her cousin was her weekly session with Afzal in a little hotel out of town. Her mother didn't know that she was on the pill; that's why there was no grandchild yet. Kamal had no idea, but occasionally, he would see her leave the house to visit her friend Rehana and wondered why she was fully made up and wearing her best clothes to see another woman.

As her mother continued to pressure her, Kulsum decided she would talk to him tonight and find out what the problem was. She knew she could seduce him easily, so that day, she went full out and had her legs and arms waxed, and for good measure, threw in a Hollywood, painful but necessary. Plus, she was due to see Afzal on Wednesday hence the preparation. She put on her favourite Britney Spears perfume, a lovely sheer white silk nightie and slipped into bed beside him. He could smell her before she got into bed, but he pretended to be asleep.

What Will Be

'I know you're not asleep Kamal, come on, talk to me.' She snuggled into him, and he turned to face her, looking tired and miserable. At that moment, she felt sorry for him. 'Come on, what's wrong?'

'Nothing, now can I go to sleep?'

'Oh no, you don't,' she said. She hadn't gone to all this trouble just for him to turn over and go to sleep. She caressed him and played with him until he grew hard under her expert hands. He made love to her savagely, but at the same time with a tenderness he hadn't displayed before. She was confident he would tell her what was wrong afterwards. He wasn't a bad lover, she thought, as she lost herself in her own fantasies.

She wasn't sure, but she thought she heard him whisper, 'Oh Amina.' Who the hell was Amina? He kissed her then leant over to get tissues from the box on the bedside table. He handed her a tissue, which she ignored. 'Who is Amina?'

'What?' he asked stupidly, completely shocked. How did she know about Amina?

'Who is Amina?'

'I, er, who, how, er.'

'You just called out her name.'

'Did I, when?'

'Just now.'

He had no recollection of that. Oh shit.

'Who is she, Kamal? And don't bother lying.'

So, he told her. Everything.

'You lying son of a bitch! Here I was thinking I was the baddie for having had a boyfriend, and all this time, you were hankering after your ex-girlfriend!'

Although she didn't love him, she felt strangely hurt and betrayed; he was her husband, after all. Her inner voice told her she had no right to feel that way, she was sleeping with her boyfriend, but she couldn't help it; it made her feel less of a woman. She had naively assumed she was his first, the irony completely bypassing her. He had told her that Amina was now living in London, too close for comfort.

What Will Be

Even though she didn't love him, she didn't want him to leave her. A divorced woman was treated with the utmost disdain and suspicion in the community. But if Kamal ever found out about Afzal, she knew that would be the end.

He had so much pride, and she was sure that would give him the excuse he needed to divorce her.

She resolved there and then to give up the man she loved and try for a baby with the one she didn't. No good would come of it, and Afzal would never leave his wife and children anyway. He was seen as a pillar of the community. If their affair ever came out, both would be ostracised and ruined, especially her.

In her community, Afzal's shame would eventually die down. Unfairly, hers would continue forever, the blame always firmly at her feet. If she was nicer to Kamal and became the lovely wife that he deserved, that had brought him all the way from Africa, then maybe he wouldn't divorce her.

She calmed down. 'It's OK, Kamal, we'll put this behind us. Everyone has a past, me included. But, we're married, we have to forget the past and concentrate on our future. Maybe Mum is right; we should concentrate all our efforts on trying for a baby. Then we can be a proper family, and I will be a better wife to you, Kamal. I promise.'

He said nothing but was pleased to see her softer, caring side. She was right; he had to forget Amina and learn to live without her in his head all the time.

London, UK

Ayan finished her college course in the summer, and Amina was thought well enough to end therapy. Although Ayan had good grades, she had decided against going to university. She had had enough of studying. She told her sister she didn't want to go to university and promptly got a job at a recruitment agency. She would learn on the job; she told Amina and would progress through the ranks this way.

Amina had got a really good job with an advertising agency, but unfortunately, it was not in London. It was in Southampton, and the company was willing to relocate her and help her find accommodation.

The sisters decided that Ayan would stay in the London flat. They would see each other at weekends as Southampton was only an hour and ten minutes away on the train. Amina invited Ayan to go to Southampton with her to check out the company's accommodation and help her move in.

Southampton, UK

'Where even is Southampton?' Ayan asked her sister as they boarded the train from Waterloo Station. She only knew London and had never ventured outside the capital.

'It's in Hampshire, and the region is often referred to as the English Riviera. Southampton itself is a small city, but it has a reputation as an international maritime city. Cruise ships from all over the world come and go from there.'

The train pulled into Southampton Central, and they made their way out. There was a taxi rank right in front of the station, and one immediately pulled up. To their great surprise, the driver was Somali. He also recognised them as fellow Somalis and greeted them warmly. It was true, Ayan thought. Somalis everywhere recognise each other, and tied by a common language, culture, and religion, always looked out for each other, especially in foreign lands. They were united against the 'Gaal,' the white man, the unbeliever, and the infidel in foreign lands.

They suppressed or hid their hatred of clans that fought and killed their relatives in Somalia. 'Welcome to Southampton sisters,' he said smiling. 'Where am I taking you?'

'The address I have is Ocean Village,' said Amina.

He whistled softly.

'What is it, brother? Is it a bad place? You see, I don't know this city at all. My company found me the flat.'

'Oh, no, don't worry, sister, it's one of the best areas of the city, right on the marina.'

He drove through the city to the marina, where they gaped at the many yachts moored and the grey waters of the Solent. The taxi driver told them that the area had recently been refurbished, with new flats overlooking the water, new bars, restaurants, and cinemas. He stopped outside a high-rise and said, 'This is it. Your new home!' He said it with great pride, as though some of the girls' success had somehow rubbed off on him. They paid him and took the lift to the 15th floor.

What Will Be

The corridor to Amina's flat looked clean and well-kept, unlike the one in Westbourne Grove, which was often grimy and musty. The two bedroomed flat was fully furnished, light, airy and spacious. Ayan ran immediately over to the floor-to-ceiling windows in the lounge and looked out to the water. 'This is lovely, sis. So quiet, but Southampton feels a bit boring, don't you think?'

Amina laughed. 'You've only been here five minutes, and you've made up your mind about the place! I'm sure it's not that bad. Come and have a look at your bedroom, where you'll be staying when you come to visit me, and it better be every weekend!'

Amina's bedroom had a double bed, and the room she assigned to her sister had two single beds.

With a small bathroom and a well-equipped kitchen, she thought the flat was perfect. 'Let's go and explore the area before you leave,' Amina suggested.

They took the lift down and walked along the marina, admiring the yachts and small boats. They found a restaurant by the waterfront where they stopped for coffee and cake, and as they sat and enjoyed their surroundings, Amina felt at peace for the first time in months. She hoped she would be happy here and couldn't wait to start her new job the following week.

When Ayan left to go back to London, Amina felt lonely and teary, but the loneliness gave her the time and space to focus on the new job. The office was based in the city centre, in a gorgeous Georgian building. She was shown to her office, which she shared with three other women, two young and one old. Everyone seemed friendly, and she thought she'd be happy here.

Chapter 19

Leicester, UK

Kamal was happier now that his wife was kinder and nicer to him. He reciprocated by buying her little presents occasionally, which she accepted with great enthusiasm. They made love often, but she still wasn't pregnant. 'Don't worry, these things take time,' he consoled her.

'But it's taking too long, Kamal. I should be pregnant by now.'

'Relax, it will happen, Insha'Allah.'

But Kulsum was worried. Her friend, who had just got married, was already pregnant. She needed to have a baby, to help her forget Afzal completely and to feel closer to Kamal. Maybe there was something wrong with her or with Kamal. She would make an appointment with the doctor to see what was wrong. Kamal agreed he would go with her, but he knew there was nothing wrong with him. She was the one who was unable to conceive.

His thoughts turned again to Amina and the baby he made her abort with an aching heart. 'Please God, don't punish me for that,' he prayed silently. Whenever he thought of Amina, he also thought of Africa, his home. What he wouldn't give to be back there, without a care in the world!

Driving a taxi in Leicester was no fun, but that was the only job he could get, the only other alternative was to work in a Bangladeshi restaurant but he couldn't bring himself to do that. Instead of working for, and relying on his father's money, he now wished he had studied harder in school and had attained some academic qualifications. Like the British Asians, he should have become a doctor, a lawyer, or an accountant, then he wouldn't be doing a shitty driving job for a living.

To add insult to his injured pride was the abuse he suffered in the taxi which always shook him.

'Filthy Paki' was often a parting shot, and he'd lost count of the number of times his passengers hot-footed it out of the taxi without paying. What disgusted him, even more were the very young white girls out on the town with skimpy clothes even at extreme temperatures. Mostly they were already drunk before getting into the taxi, and a few times, he had to offload them before their destination as one would invariably vomit. He often asked

What Will Be

himself where the parents were, how could they let their young daughters go out looking like mini hookers? Oh yes, he knew what hookers looked like, he had had plenty in his taxi, but they were always polite and paid their fare.

In Africa, he was treated with respect, but he was treated like shit in the UK. His parents thought he was happy, living in the UK, the Promised Land for Indians, and Pakistanis. If only they knew, they were not wanted here, not a day goes by when he doesn't hear 'go home Paki!' And the funny thing was, given half the chance, they would go home, him to Africa and his in-laws to Pakistan.

The more one stayed in the UK, the more attractive the motherland became. Maybe he could persuade Kulsum to go back to Africa with him. He'd never discussed this with her, but he had a feeling she would say no. The UK wasn't the nirvana it was made out to be. When he was in Kenya, many of his friends had gone to universities in the UK, and whole families had moved there, believing they'd have a better life.

He saw some of these families now, in the small, dingy terraced houses that couldn't house a family of more than four. They had left their own villas and luxurious lifestyle for a promised land that treated them as second or even third-class citizens, the butt of jokes and abuse. In Kenya, they used to insult and abuse the Africans who they had always treated as second-class citizens. Now they were getting a taste of their own medicine, and they didn't like it one bit.

Almost every foreign man Kamal knew in Leicester was a taxi driver or a waiter. They simply couldn't find other decent jobs. Of course, they had tried, but the rejection letter was quick to follow once the employer saw the foreign name. Even when they cottoned on and anglicised their names, they were rejected after the interview, when Mr Smith, interviewing, realised that Mr Caan, the interviewee, was not white.

Kamal had been appalled that men in his community changed their names and adopted Christian ones. At his taxi firm, he met many Pakistani men. He was appalled once to hear the controller call one Ass and him cheerfully responding. 'What did he just call you?' Kamal asked.

'Ass, it's my name.'

'Your name is Ass?'

'Yes.'

What Will Be

'What is your Muslim name?'

'Asaad'

'Do you know what it means, your name?'

'No.'

'It means lion, and here you are, allowing someone to call you an ass! How shameful!'

'But it's easier for them to pronounce than Asaad.'

'Keep telling yourself that, donkey! Did your boss change his English name to make it easier for you to pronounce?'

The Pakistanis weren't the only ones changing names, though. He had also noticed that Somali people were doing the same. The female Fadumo became Fay and Mohamed, the greatest name a Muslim male could have, became Mo or Max as Bilal became Billy. He felt sad that these beautiful Muslim names were now being eradicated slowly by the same people who should be doing everything to preserve them. He had resisted his name being shortened to Kam, adding the al if someone called Kam. He hoped Amina wouldn't change her name, like the Aminas he knew through his in-laws who called themselves Amy.

He wondered what she was doing now and whether she was happy. She popped into his head at least once a day. Shaking her off, he rushed off for his evening prayer. He attended mosque regularly now; it has become his solace and only salvation. In Nairobi, he never went, now goes just to get away from the house he shares with his wife and her family. He and his wife were still in one room after all this time; how he was ever going to get enough money to buy a house, God only knew.

After the mosque, he goes home for dinner, which is already on the table. His aunt and mother-in-law is the chief cook, with Kulsum sometimes helping. He greets his aunt with a kiss and goes to wash his hands.

Kulsum corners him by the sink and says, 'By the way, I've made an appointment for us at the doctors. Tomorrow at ten.'

'Oh, OK,' he agrees as he goes to the table.

The food is always good, lovely chicken biriyani, mutton curry and hot chapattis.

'My friend Shamim's daughter just had a baby boy,' the aunt informed everyone. Meaningfully, she looked at her daughter, who rolled her eyes.

What Will Be

'Oh Mummy, how many friends have you got? You tell us about a new baby every week!'

'Well, I'm jealous. I want to be a grandma too!'

'You will be inshallah, Auntie.'

His uncle, a man of few words, said to his wife, 'Don't put pressure on them. Only Allah knows when a baby will come.'

London, UK

Back in London, Ayan was missing her sister. London suddenly felt cold and unfriendly. The flat seemed empty without her sister. She had friends, but they were not a substitute for her sister. Besides, she still worried about Amina after her PTSD diagnosis. They spoke on the phone every day, Amina telling her sister all about the job and the new friends she had made. She also told her about the old woman in her office who seemed to dislike her.

'Not everybody's going to like you, sis. Just ignore her,' she told Amina on the phone.

'Very difficult to ignore her when she's sitting in front of me! I've found out she is quite unpopular with the staff.' She left Ayan in giggles as she told her how the old woman often farted, even at meetings, and would say, unembarrassed, 'excuse me'!

Ayan, however, enjoyed her job at the recruitment agency. She loved helping people find jobs, and her reward was the happiness that shone out of the clients' faces when they realised they were no longer unemployed. She worked long hours, but she didn't mind. After work, she went to the gym or met up with some of her friends. Weekends, if she wasn't going to Southampton, she spent with her Somali friends. Although she loved going to their homes and was always warmly welcomed by the family, she still felt lonely and bereft. Alone in the flat at night, her thoughts turned to her camp mother Anab and her own mother, who she could barely remember. Sometimes at her friend's house, a certain smell would transport her back home to Somalia; she didn't know whether it was her mum or her dad's scent. But it was so familiar, she often couldn't bear it and walked out of the house.

Southampton, UK

What Will Be

When Amina next saw her, she noticed that her little sister didn't look too happy. She thought she'd cheer her up by taking her to the cinema. Ever since she was a child, Ayan had loved films, both Bollywood and Hollywood. 'We're going to watch that new film you told me about, then we'll grab dinner somewhere nice. Southampton's Oxford Street has some nice trendy restaurants, although I haven't seen any Arab or Somali restaurants.'

After the film at Leisure World, which they both enjoyed, they went to an Indian restaurant. 'This is the closest to Somali food we'll get!' Amina told her sister, laughing. The restaurant had an a la carte menu and a buffet, and they opted for the buffet. 'I've eaten here before; their samosas are to die for! Here, have this one; I prefer the meat one to the veggie one.'

'Mmm, it's good,' agreed Ayan, stuffing the tasty pastry in her mouth. 'So, tell me what's been happening in London since I left?'

'Since you left the big city for a village, you mean?'

'Oh, stop it! Southampton is hardly a village; it's quite a big city.'

'If you say so. Anyway, nothing much has changed in London, same old, same old.'

'Oh yeah? Why do you seem so miserable then? Are we in love?'

'Stop it, I'm not in love. Besides, I have no time to think about boys; I'm too busy at work.'

'OK, then, what gives? You've always been able to talk to me about anything.'

'If you must know, I feel lonely all the time, even when I'm with people. And lately, I've been thinking a lot about Anab and our mum.'

'Oh hon, you're missing them, of course, you are, and it's only natural.' Ayan's eyes welled up, 'I don't remember our mum's face, and yes, I miss her and Anab.'

'I miss them too, sweetie, and I understand; Anab became our mum for all the years when we fled Mogadishu.'

'We don't even know what happened to her. Is she dead or alive? Amina, how can we both live happily in the UK when that poor woman who looked after us is still suffering somewhere? We were her only 'relatives.'

'I've often thought of her too, sis. I'll tell you what, I'll make inquiries and see what we can find. I know someone who works for the Red Cross,

What Will Be

and they have a family reunion programme. I've heard that some Somalis here have been reunited with their families through the Red Cross.'

'Oh, would you, sis? That'd be brilliant!' Seeing the happiness on her sister's face almost made Amina cry, and she vowed silently that she would do all she could to find out what happened to their foster mother.

True to her word, Amina wasted no time in trying to trace Anab. On Monday, at work, she rang the woman she knew at the Red Cross and got an immediate appointment to see someone.

At the appointment, she was asked several questions about Anab, her full name, age. She couldn't answer all the questions, especially about Anab's age. 'I really don't know how old she is or was; I just know she wasn't young.

The adviser said, 'Not to worry, we'll work with what we have. First things, first. We have to fill this form in. Yeah, I know, it's long, but if we do it together, we should be done in no time.' She showed Amina a road map of the family reunion process. She explained that the first step was gathering evidence, followed by lots of form filling, making the application, preparing for the embassy interview, and finally attending the appointment. It was daunting, but Amina remembered her promise to Ayan, which gave her the strength and determination to find Anab.

The adviser told her that she would try to locate Anab. She would get the Red Cross representative in Kenya to check the refugee camp and see if she was still there. Amina asked about payment, and the adviser told her family reunion applications were free. 'How long will all this take?' she asked.

'Well, first we have to find Anab and see if she's still in the old camp or moved elsewhere. After that, we will start the process of getting her to the UK. That will take at least three months.'

'OK, thanks, here's my card, just let me know when you hear anything, please.'

Work was going splendidly for Amina until she was told to work on a major client with one of the other ladies in the public relations department. This was with the oldest of the four of them who made up the department. Amina got on well with the other two, but not with this old lady, who she didn't particularly warm to. She silently cursed her boss for pairing her off with the harridan.

As she had found out, this woman was very unpopular with almost everyone in the company. Even her name was old, Althea, and caused a few titters at client introductions. As she explained to Ayan, she also had the unfortunate habit of passing wind regularly and without embarrassment, even at meetings. She would simply say, 'Sorry.'

This explained why at Christmas, secret Santa always gave her a whoopee cushion. She had affected what she thought was a posh English accent, but it just made her sound like an old colonial headmistress in Kenya. Whenever they went for the client meeting, she would take over and not give Amina a chance to say anything. As soon as they got back to the office, she would give Amina the task of writing up the contact reports, filing and any other mundane jobs she could find.

Day to day, Althea kept giving Amina all her dirty work while reaping the rewards herself. Amina restrained herself often and told herself it was only temporary. However, her behaviour worsened, making Amina wonder if this woman was simply a racist or just evil by nature. So, one day, she asked her casually, 'Have you ever been to Africa?'

She was surprised by the answer. 'Oh yes, I love Africa. I go to the Gambia every year. The people are lovely, especially the men, know what I mean?'

Amina was horrified. Was this woman one of those she had read about in the papers, old white ladies who go to Africa for sun and sex? She was divorced, and she had two grown-up daughters. 'Er, no, I don't know what you mean,' she blustered and walked away. Well, that put paid to her racist theory!

Usually, someone got up and offered to make tea or coffee for the others in the team. Amina decided she would specifically ask Althea if she could make her a cup of tea. 'I'm going to the tea room. Would you like a cuppa, Althea?'

'Oh, yes, please, milk, no sugar.'

Amina went to the small kitchenette, filled the kettle, and put out two mugs. She made herself an instant coffee and made a cup of tea for Althea. Before she took the mugs back, she spat several times in the mug, stirred it, and thought, 'I'll get that old bitch! Let her drink my spit!'

What Will Be

'Here you go, Althea,' she said sweetly and smiled inwardly when she saw her take a sip of her tea, without so much as a thank you. However, in bed that night, she wondered how she could have done such a thing, it was pure evil, but it taught her something valuable; she vowed from then on never to accept anyone's offer of tea. She decided to be nicer to Althea, even though she couldn't stand her. All this, however, changed the next morning.

Althea walked to Amina's desk and slammed some files hard onto her desk. 'Work on these,' she ordered and walked back to her desk.

A red mist descended upon Amina's eyes. She picked up the files, walked over to Althea's desk and slammed them down hard on her desk.

'What the hell are you doing?' Althea asked.

'I'm doing what I should have done months ago. Never, ever, ever, ever, do that again. I am not your lackey, you stupid, old bitch!'

'Don't point your finger in my face,' said Althea.

Incensed, Amina stuck her finger on her forehead, pushed hard and said, 'I'll do more than that to you. Who the hell do you think you are? I've kept my mouth shut and my temper in check for months. But enough is enough. In Africa, we respect our elders, which I tried to do with you, but you don't deserve any respect. Do what you did to me again, and I'll have your fucking head, you bitch!'

Shaken, Althea got up and took off while the others in the office were stunned into silence. They had never seen Amina lose her temper before and it was frightening. Amina felt good; no silly old white woman was going to ever disrespect her again. Minutes later, her phone rang, the boss wanted to see her. She knew Althea would go running to him. She went to his office, still fuming. 'I'll resign; you don't have to fire me', she said, beyond caring now.

'No-one's going to fire you. Althea has been here, and she told me what happened,' he said, surprisingly smiling. 'Go round the block for a walk and cool off. We'll talk about this later.'

Amina was relieved and left the office to clear her head. When she got back to the office, everyone, all two hundred employees, knew what had happened because her team had sent emails around. People from different departments came up to her to congratulate her.

What Will Be

'Bravo, she deserved it, the stupid cow!'

The boss later called both of them to the office to make up.

Althea started. 'I'm sorry I made you feel inferior.'

What? Amina was incensed, the arrogant bitch, time to deflate her ego. She smiled sweetly at her and replied, 'You can never make me feel inferior. How can you? In fact, I feel superior to you; I'm younger, slimmer, prettier and with two degrees! What have you got apart from a stinky dog and daughters who don't even like you?'

The boss, who also clearly disliked the woman but had to be impartial, could not suppress a smile at that. 'Try and get along, you two, I'm going to assign different accounts for you' he said and shooed them out of his office.

From then on, Althea was as good as gold and treated Amina with great caution. A few months later, she gave a box of chocolates to Amina at her retirement party, which surprised her. Her boss said, 'She wants you to get fat.'

'They're going straight in the bin! She's probably poisoned them!' With Althea, gone, the office became a more relaxed and friendly place to work. Amina began enjoying her work once more and was working hard to earn a promotion. She wanted to be Head of Department which would enable her to earn more money so she could buy herself a flat.

Chapter 20

Amina was enjoying her job and her life. She had made many friends in Southampton and often went out with them. She was with a group of girls when she met Dylan. The club was in Leisure World, where she often watched films at the Odeon with her friends. He was with a group of friends, and he kept glancing back at her.

Andrea, one of her friends, noticed and said, 'That guy's checking you out, Amina, and gosh, is he gorgeous! Go on and smile back at him, girl!'

'No, I won't, stop it. He's probably looking at one of you. I know white men prefer blondes.'

When he noticed the girl's gestures and giggles, he knew they were talking about him. 'It's now or never,' he thought as he strolled up to them, looked straight at Amina and asked, 'Can I buy you a drink? I'm Dylan, by the way.'

'I don't drink,' she replied.

He countered, 'Everybody drinks; you mean you don't drink alcohol.'

'Yes, that's what I meant.'

'Well then, can I buy you a non-alcoholic drink?'

Nudged by her friends, she agreed. 'Diet coke, please.'

While he went to get the drink, the girls continued to encourage Amina.

'Yeah, yeah, OK, it's not as if I hadn't noticed he's good looking.'

When he came back with the drink, he said, 'Here you go. Now please at least tell me your name.'

'Amina.'

'Oh, that's a nice name. Where's it from?'

'It's Arabic. It means the trustworthy one.'

'So, you're Arab?'

'No, I'm Somali, from Somalia.'

'In East Africa, or more specifically, the Horn of Africa?' he replied.

'Wow, I'm impressed! Not many people know where Somalia is or who Somalis are. I've lost count of the number of times I've been mistaken for an Indian, a Filipino, anything but a Somali.'

'Well, I like travelling and getting to know about different countries, cultures and religions.'

'Not your typical Englishman then,' she teased.

'No, definitely not!' he laughed.

They found themselves isolated and still chatting away easily when one of her friends came up to her and said, 'We've got to call it a night. Are you coming or not?'

'What, already?' asked Amina.

'It's four o'clock in the morning, dear.'

Amina was shocked, she hadn't realised it was that late and that she had spent hours chatting to this stranger that she had just met. 'I'm sorry, I've got to go,' she said reluctantly.

Dylan was equally reluctant to let her go, but he produced a business card and gave it to her. 'Please ring me,' he pleaded. 'I'd like to see you again.'

'Me too,' she admitted and gave him one of her cards.

On Monday, a huge bouquet of flowers arrived for her, signed Dylan, with a simple message, 'So lovely meeting you last night. I can't stop thinking about you.'

Amina was pleased because she couldn't stop thinking about him either. She had been daydreaming about him most of the day and had to force herself to concentrate on her work. She remembered his dark curly hair and beautiful green eyes. It had been a long time since someone made her heart flutter.

The girls in the office teased her mercilessly, but she didn't mind. She rang him and thanked him for the flowers and arranged to meet him on Wednesday for dinner. He took her to Kutis, and she asked, 'how did you know I like Indian food?'

'I don't know, I just thought that you wouldn't want fish and chips on a first date.'

'Well, you're right. I love Indian food anyway; it reminds me of the food we used to have back in Somalia.'

What Will Be

That night was the same as the first night they met. They talked nonstop until they discovered all they could about each other. She told him about Somalia, the refugee camp, and her journey to the UK.

He was absolutely fascinated and mesmerised by this exotic beauty. He told her about himself. He was an only child of doting parents. He had been to university in the north and started his own investment company a couple of years later.

He was clearly successful, judging by his designer watch, shoes, and clothes, not to mention some expensive aftershave.

She liked that he was humble and not arrogant like some of the other men she met.

Soon they were an item, Dylan, and Amina. She introduced him to her sister Ayan who expressed slight disapproval. He took her home to introduce her to his parents, and while she loved the dad, the mum was not exactly her cup of tea. The dad was very welcoming and asked her questions about herself.

The mum was cold and distant, and even when she smiled, her fake smile did not reach her eyes, but her son was oblivious to this, all his attention on his new girlfriend. 'Did you have food like this in Africa?' she asked Amina.

'Yes,' she replied politely. Did the woman think she came from another planet? The dinner was nothing special; either his mother was a bad cook, or she simply hadn't bothered. She had served up dry, boiled chicken, boiled potatoes, and overcooked boiled cauliflower. There was no salt or pepper on the table to flavour the food, and although Amina ate it to be polite, she felt like throwing up.

'I hope he doesn't invite me to his parents' house for dinner again,' she prayed silently.

Still, she was happy she had survived the meeting and had the father, at least, on her side. Even at this early stage in their relationship, she already knew there would be a battle between her and the mother.

Ayan still came to visit her sister regularly. Although she was in love and wrapped up with Dylan, Amina noticed that Ayan was becoming increasingly religious while she was becoming increasingly rebellious.

What Will Be

On the phone to Amina one day, she said, 'And, by the way, you shouldn't be having a boyfriend. It's haram; if he loves you as you say, you should make it halal and get married.'

'We've only just met, and we certainly haven't talked about marriage! You're nuts; people don't get married after a couple of months.'

'Muslims do.'

'Well, he's not a Muslim.'

'But you are.'

'Oh, for God's sake Ayan, stop this, I'm not getting married! Besides, I have more important things to think about.'

'Like what?'

'Like Anab.'

'What, have you heard anything from or about her?'

'I'm not sure, but the adviser at the Red Cross called me and asked me to go see her, so I'm hoping she'll have some information; I'll let you know what she says.'

On Monday morning, she walked through the park from her office on Grosvenor Square to the Red Cross office in the city centre. The adviser greeted her warmly as Amina sat down anxiously. 'Any news?' she asked.

'Yes, good news, in fact. Anab has been located at a different refugee camp in Kenya. As she is listed as having no living relatives, no one has claimed her or bothered to get her out of the camp. Since you claim she is your mother, we will have to do a DNA test to prove this before we can do anything further.'

'Did I not tell you? She is not our blood mother; our blood mother was murdered in Mogadishu. Anab took us in and looked after us as though she had given birth to us. We consider her our mother because she cared for and loved us all those years when we were by ourselves in the camp. She has no one, you said so yourself, she's been left behind in the camp, but we're here now. We want to claim her as our mother and bring her here to be with us.'

'OK, we will have to apply under extenuating circumstances then.'

Amina was so happy that the Red Cross had at last found Anab. She had feared the worst, that Anab was either dead or removed from the camp to some obscure country by the UNHCR. She had been moved to anoth-

What Will Be

er camp, Utanga Refugee Camp, where she thought she would end her remaining years of life. Amina conveyed the good news to her sister, who cried with happiness.

Over the next few weeks, the Red Cross arranged for Anab to acquire travel documents through their office in Kenya, followed by interviews at the British High Commission in Nairobi. Anab had been alerted that two sisters who claimed she was their mother were searching for her and wanted her to come to the UK to live with them. When she heard this, she had burst into tears. 'Yes, they're my daughters; I never thought I would ever see or hear from them again. I thought they had forgotten all about me, although I've never forgotten them and think about them almost every day. I'm so glad they're alive and well.'

Amina and Ayan were interviewed separately at the Red Cross in London. They were asked to provide all sorts of documents. Thank God Amina had a good job; she brought along her payslips and showed photos of her apartment where Anab would stay when she came.

A few weeks later, the adviser informed Amina that the application for the family reunion was successful and that a date had been set for Anab to come to the UK. Since she had never been on a plane before and spoke no English, an official from the Red Cross in Kenya would fly with her to the UK.

Both Amina and Ayan wanted to meet her off the plane and waited patiently for KQ Flight 786 to land at Heathrow airport. Ayan had brought a bunch of flowers which Amina thought was a useless but sweet gesture. She had come prepared with a large winter coat, so Anab wouldn't get a shock when the cold winter air hit her for the first time.

They watched as people rushed out of the arrivals lounge, searching for Anab. A tall Somali man emerged, leading a thin, old lady by the hand. At first, they didn't register, then suddenly it dawned on them that this must be Anab. They rushed to her, and although it took a while for Anab to recognise the girls, they were all soon hugging and crying with happiness.

The Somali man introduced himself as the Red Cross worker tasked with bringing Anab over to the UK. He established who they were and bid farewell to all of them. His job as an escort was done.

Amina and Ayan told Anab to wear her coat which was clearly too big and swamped her small body. They were shortly going outside to take the National Express to Southampton. They walked slowly because Anab couldn't walk very fast until they got to the bus terminal. Luckily, the 302 to Southampton was already there, and they waited in line to board. The journey would take around two and a half hours, and Anab slept most of that time, waking from time to time to gaze at the girls in wonder.

Amina and Ayan kept looking at her too, not believing that she was actually here, with them. When the bus finally arrived at the bus station in Southampton, Amina hailed a taxi to take them to her flat.

'The sea,' said Anab when they got to Ocean Village. 'You live by the sea; it's so pretty here. I haven't seen the sea since Somalia.'

They spent the afternoon catching up with each other, with Anab gazing at both of them in awe. 'You have grown into beautiful women, and I still can't believe you found me. I missed you so much after you left.'

'We missed you too, Mum, but now that we've found you, we're never letting you go. You will stay with me; Ayan has to go back to London tomorrow.'

'Why, doesn't she live here with you? This place is big enough for all of us.'

'Mum, I have my own place in London. A flat that I share with my sisters.'

'Your sisters? I thought Amina was your only sister.'

'Oh, she means her sisters in Islam,' Amina explained with a smile. 'She was lonely when I left, so she got two other girls to take my room.'

The weekend passed by happily and quickly. The sisters took Anab shopping, and she looked in wonder at the big shopping malls. They went to John Lewis, where they kitted her up with sweaters, thermal underwear, scarves, and sturdy winter boots. 'Don't spend all your money on me,' she protested, but they told her not to worry and that she really needed everything they were buying her.

'The winters in Southampton are not harsh, but for you, it will be cold because you're not used to it. We will also register you with a doctor because you will need a flu jab. People over sixty get it free here.'

'I don't need any jabs, child. I'm fine.'

'No, Mum, believe me, you will need this one; all older people get them here.'

What Will Be

Soon it was time for a very happy Ayan to go back to London, and she took the last train to Waterloo, with promises that she would come as often as she could.

Amina resumed work on Monday, happy in the knowledge that her mum would be home when she finished work and that she wouldn't be going to an empty flat anymore. At work, she called the flat several times to check that Anab was OK.

Anab told her to stop worrying and informed her that she had also received several phone calls from Ayan.

'Do your jobs, don't keep checking up on me like I'm a child. I'm fine; I can look after myself.'

The months passed, and true to her word, Ayan came as often as possible, and the trio became more comfortable and settled in Southampton.

One day Anab asked Amina whether there were any other Somalis in the city.

'I'm sure there are; they are everywhere,' Amina replied. 'Remember that taxi driver who brought us home from the station? He was Somali. Why?'

'Because I feel lonely sometimes, especially with you gone all day, and I have nothing to do. Once I finish cooking and cleaning, I just sit and stare.'

'But you don't have to clean, you know I have someone who comes to clean once a week, and I can do the cooking when I get back, or we'll get a takeaway.'

'But I have to keep busy, Amina. Even if I switch the TV on, I can't enjoy it because I don't understand what they're saying.'

'That's an easy one to solve Mum, I'll get satellite TV where you can watch Somali channels.'

'That's good, but I still don't want to be sitting here watching TV all day, every day by myself.'

'OK, Mum, I'll make inquiries and see if they have Somali groups in the city.'

Her search led her to the Southampton Somali Association, set up when the city started accepting Somali asylum seekers and refugees. She found

What Will Be

out that their office was in Northam, bang in the middle of countless council high rise blocks.

In her lunch hour, she went to their office and met one of the two workers there. She introduced herself, and he led her to a side office, opposite of which sat several Somali men, chatting and drinking tea. There wasn't a woman in sight. 'I've come to ask if you have women's meetings here.'

'Yes, we do, we have a sewing class and an English language class. Do you want to enrol?'

'Oh no, it's not for me, it's for my mum, but I don't think she'll want to do sewing or English, she just wants something sociable, like meeting other women her age over tea.'

'I see. May I ask what clan she is?'

Amina was shocked. 'What? Why do you want to know her clan?'

He shifted uncomfortably, 'It's just so I can put her in touch with people from her own clan.'

Amina was shouting now, and the men in the opposite office were becoming interested in the conversation. 'I'm certainly not going to tell you which clan she is. How dare you? This clans talk is nonsense, and to find you here, in the UK, propagating such rubbish, it's beyond incredible. I've checked you out; you're funded by the government, right? Well, I'm going to complain to them and tell them you're divisive.'

She stormed out of the office, but before she got to the car park, one of the men caught up with her. 'Listen, sister, don't pay any attention to Askar. He's full of shit; the association is for all clans, not just his, although he doesn't quite comprehend this. Plus, I know old ladies get lonely; it's not like back home when they had family surrounding them all the time. It's very difficult for the elderly in this country, feeling quite isolated, leading to mental health problems. I know, because I also have an old aunt who lives with me. Maybe we could introduce the two?'

Amina calmed down. 'That's a great idea, thank you. When shall we do this?'

'Anytime you like, it's not as if my aunt is going anywhere.'

'No time like the present,' she replied.

'My name's Ali, by the way.'

'Amina.'

What Will Be

'My taxi is right over there, and I promise I won't ask your clan,' he joked.

Amina smiled. 'It just makes me so mad, Ali. My parents were both murdered in Somalia, and just when I thought I was free from clan hatred, it rears its ugly head here.'

'Some people never change, Amina. But we have to rise above that. We are all Somalis. Do you know we are probably the only nation in the world with one language, one culture and one religion? Yet we are at each other's throats, both here and at home, utter madness.'

Amina gave him her address, and they drove there to get Anab. Ali waited downstairs as she went into the lift.

Anab was worried about seeing Amina. 'Are you ill? Why aren't you at work?'

'I'm fine, Mum. I just came to take you out, to introduce you to a Somali lady.'

In the taxi, she introduced Ali, who greeted her respectfully. He drove them to Derby Road, which Ali informed her had a few Somali families but that the area was mainly Asian. He stopped outside a small terraced house, opened the door, and ushered them in. 'Welcome, Aunt, to my house. I'll just go get my aunt.' He led them to a tiny sitting room, quite dingy and dark, the curtains still closed. He drew the curtains apologetically. 'Auntie thinks that people will see her.'

The aunt, a tall, thin lady, clapped her hands gleefully when she saw Amina and Anab. 'Aah, visitors!'

Ali made the introductions, then left to make tea. He came back with tea, biscuits, and fruit juice.

The ladies were chatting away happily, so Ali took his leave. 'I can see I'm not much use here, so I better go earn my living. Amina, can I drive you back to work, or will you be staying?' He corrected himself quickly. 'Oh, I forgot you left your car in Northam, I'll drive you back there.'

She glanced at Anab, who shooed her away. 'You youngsters go, we'll be just fine.'

So began a friendship for both Amina and Anab, who never complained about being lonely again. She got into the habit of being collected by Ali on his taxi rounds every day and being taken to her new friend's house. She spent many happy hours drinking tea or coffee and talking about Somalia's 'good old days'. Sometimes they would be visited by some of the younger women in the community who brought back all the community news and gossip. Whose husband has married a second wife, who has gone back to the old country, injustices, racism, the benefits system, the list was endless! Still, the old ladies enjoyed all this gossip. It was a window to the outside world, and the younger women felt they were doing their duty by looking in on the elderly. Some of them had lost their own mothers and came to look upon the old ladies as surrogate mums or grandmothers.

Asha, one of the younger women, started her tale of the day. 'I went to West Quay the other day, looking for some things to buy for the children. As soon as I entered the shop, the salesgirl clocked me and started following me around. I ignored this for a while, but she was really getting on my nerves. Why are you following me? I asked angrily. She went bright red; she was only a young girl. 'Well?' I said.

She mumbled something, and I said I didn't understand and could she repeat what she'd said.

'I'm going to get in trouble if anyone hears me say this,' she said, 'but management have asked us to follow anyone wearing what you're wearing.'

'What I'm wearing? What am I wearing?'

'The burka, you call it, innit?' We've had shoplifting episodes in the shop, and we've caught culprits hiding items under their clothes.'

The other ladies were shocked and started speaking all at once. 'Which shop was it? I'll never go there. Just because we wear the shuko doesn't mean we are all thieves!'

'It is ignorance, coupled with racism, just because we're Muslims!'

Warming up to her subject, Asha continued. 'That's not all. Do you know even the police in Southampton are racist? My husband told me that the Somali taxi drivers are always stopped by police to check their documents. At the same time, their white colleagues are waved off. Can you imagine that?'

'There's nothing we can do about that. We're the ones who made a choice to come to their country. They did not invite us,' said Amal, a mother of six who had recently relocated from Sweden.

'The other day, the headteacher at my children's school asked me why we had come to the UK. She said Sweden had a better education system, university was free and a very high standard of living. I told her we came here because I wanted my children to learn English and speak the language. You know what she said then? She said we didn't have to come here to learn English, we could learn it in Sweden, and the Swedes speak very good English, by the way. I just felt she was indirectly saying leave my country.'

'She's right though, and Scandinavian countries are far more generous with their benefits, but us Somalis, we just follow each other like sheep,' said Asha. 'Families are now leaving Southampton for Birmingham because they've heard it's a better place for Muslims. If someone comes and says Siberia is the place to go and the benefits are better, we would go in droves!'

'Hey, but we've always been nomads. You must remember at least one grandparent telling you about how they loaded camels with food and other provisions and went on their way across the country!'

At this juncture, the older ladies would interject with various stories.

Anab's new friend Mayran said, 'Yes, I remember going on the camel convoy with my parents. We would stop somewhere near water for both the animals and us. We would sleep under the stars, on a mat on the ground. A fire would be lit by the men that would be stoked all night. This was to keep wild animals like lions and leopards away. But I still shake with fear all these years later when I remember the roar of the lion. I can't really describe it, but it just goes right through you and leaves you shaken right to your core.'

To lighten the subject, another young lady said, 'Auntie, tell us again about when you were married.'

'Don't you ever get tired of that story?' smiled Mayran.

'No, please tell us again, it's so romantic!'

'Nothing romantic about it. A boy from the neighbouring village came to ask for my hand in marriage, but my father refused, saying I was too young. I was thirteen, and most of the girls in our village were married by fifteen. I had glimpsed him from a far, and I thought him a very handsome fellow! He didn't give up, and soon Mahamoud starting coming to our village to hang out with our boys. One of those boys was my brother Ali. He told me how kind and brave Mahamoud was, and I loved those stories, although I had to pretend, I wasn't interested. My friends all thought he was handsome too and couldn't understand why my dad had said no. So, we took to hanging around where the boys were, but a respectable distance away. You see, we weren't allowed to play or be too near boys.'

'Come on, Auntie, get to the exciting bit!'

'So impatient. Anyway, Mahamoud and I talked over time, and I realised I loved him and didn't want to marry any other man. He said he didn't want any other girl either. So, he hatched a plan which I agreed to even though I was so scared my parents would kill me if the plan failed. He told me to wait outside our hut at midday. No one in the village had a watch, but everyone was very good at telling the time just by looking at the sun. So precisely at midday, I stopped my chores and went outside. Somalis were great horsemen then; we even fought the British on horseback and pushed them out of the country! Two white horses came thundering towards our hut, one of them ridden by Mahamoud. He smiled when he saw me, bent down, and scooped me up and away on the horse still riding furiously.

When the menfolk in our village realised what had happened, we were halfway to Mahamoud's village. Just like in the cowboy films you watch today, the men in my village, led by my father and other senior relatives, formed a posse, and rode after us. When we got to his village, we were warmly welcomed, the women ululating in the way we do at weddings. Mahamoud took me to a hut where his father and the men of the village were waiting.

An Imam was sitting with them. 'So, this is your bride; now you are our daughter. Welcome my daughter, please sit,' he said.

I sat down, and Mahamoud sat next to me on the stools provided.

'Imam, since these two want each other, and my son has effectively kidnapped her, please let us do the nikkah ceremony quickly. You know her people will be here soon to take her back, but obviously not if she's married.'

'The Imam agreed and asked me if I was sure I wanted to be married to Mahamoud. I said yes, and the groom was asked the same question. After blessing us and reading verses from the Quran, we were married.

I had envisaged a week-long wedding, being made up, henna on my hands and feet, beautiful clothes, but here I was, married with none of that but very happy. I had married the man of my dreams, who had come to get me on his white stallion. At the same time, I feared my father's wrath and waited nervously with everyone else for the posse from my village to arrive.

When they arrived, they were welcomed according to Somali tradition. You feed and look after your visitors first, and then the questions come later.

After they had rested and eaten, Mahamoud's father spoke. 'My brothers, I'm sorry we have to meet in this way. We don't want to disrespect you and your family, but our children have chosen each other. It is destiny that brought them together, and we cannot stand in their way. You, my brother Mayran's dad, I know you didn't want her to get married so young. But if they love and want each other, who are we to stand in their way? Surely Allah has chosen this path for them, and we all have to accept it. The nikkah has already taken place, and they are now man and wife in the eyes of Allah.'

My father reluctantly agreed and said they could not take me back now that I was married. I now belonged with Mahamoud's village. But a haal had to be paid. This is a sort of fine for the wrong done to a family. On top of that, my dowry was also paid, so my father went home a wealthier, if not a happier man. Mahamoud and I lived happily together until Allah took him many years later. I bore him two sons and three daughters, all good children and my pride and joy. Of course, the war took one of my sons, and my other four children live in Canada and Sweden. I chose to be with my nephew Ali because he has no one, having lost his parents in Somalia.'

All these stories were related back to Amina in the evening, giving her an insight into her community. She was so busy at work that she hadn't made any Somali friends, but she was glad at least Anab was there to talk to her in her own language and keep her up to date.

Dylan was still very attentive to her, coming up with new restaurants to try and taking her out of Southampton at weekends to places like the New Forest, Bournemouth, The Isle of Wight and Highcliffe.

She remembered laughing so hard she nearly choked when he told her the old schoolboy joke, 'What comes steaming out of Cowes? The Isle of Wight Ferry!'

When she wasn't working or with him, she went jogging around the common. She enjoyed this beautiful, open space and always felt free and happy here. Although she was happy at work, she saw no sign of progression and was becoming increasingly restless. She thought she would head the department by now, given that her boss and her clients always praised her work.

Things came to a head when a new lady was appointed head of PR, and she discovered that this lady was less qualified and less experienced than her. She went straight to her boss to complain, but he fobbed her off with some excuse.

Amina had always liked and respected her boss, but now the scales fell from her eyes. He was not the special, understanding man she had thought he was, and she came to the sad realisation that perhaps he was a racist.

'He only sees me as a workhorse who brings a lot of money to his agency,' she thought sadly.

There was absolutely no reason for her not to have had that post; even her colleagues were shocked that she hadn't been promoted. When she met Dylan that evening, he asked her what was wrong.

'Why? nothing's wrong.'

'There is, I notice every little change in you,' he laughed. So, she told him the situation at work.

He was appalled but said, 'If you don't like it, then do something about it.'

'Yeah, what?'

'Well, you could get another job, MBR who handle my advertising, are looking for people, and they're a big agency.'

'Er, no thanks, darling. As soon as I walk in, they'll say I got the job because of you! I could start my own agency, I suppose, but that'll be hard.'

'Why don't you? You'll work for yourself, no bosses, and no annoying women. I'll help in any way I can.'

The more she thought about it, the more the idea appealed to her. She started compiling a list of her favourite clients, took several out to lunch and dinner as she courted them. She told the few she trusted, under oath, not to spill the beans that she was branching out on her own. She was humbled that they didn't want her to leave but elated when a few said they would go with her. She only needed a few clients to start, and she would be walking away with her company's biggest and best.

What Will Be

Dylan gave her a small office in one of his commercial buildings, a Grade 2 listed building. He told her it was important to have an impressive address for her business.

She had already given her notice and would be leaving soon.

Her boss threw her a farewell party; he knew she was a hard worker and wished she hadn't resigned. Despite his probing, she didn't tell him where she was going next, just that she was taking time off to go back to London, spend time with her sister and think about her next move. He would soon find out anyway, Southampton was a small town.

Three months later, AAA advertising (the initials standing for Amina, Ayan and Anab) was officially launched. Dylan's office invited the press and the local business community, while Amina invited the agency's newest clients. On Monday in The Daily Echo, her boss was confronted by colourful photos of his former employee and some of his former clients.

Chapter 21

Leicester, UK

In Leicester, Kamal carried on with his mundane life. He still drove a taxi, still lived at home with his in-laws and hung his head low. Gone was the swaggering, young stud, Nairobi's heartthrob. Being in the UK had taught him he was not special after all. At home in Nairobi, he was the favoured son and never had to lift a finger. Like all Asian boys in Nairobi, he was treated like a prince, his bed made, his meals cooked, he'd throw his clothes on the floor, and he would come home to find that the maid had washed, ironed, and hung his clothes up. Now, all he had to look forward to after his shifts were dinner with the in-laws, followed by sitting on the sofa watching Pakistani TV programmes or a Bollywood film over satellite and then bed.

This sameness of this daily routine bored him along with the greasy food prepared by his mother-in-law. He needed a change. Otherwise, he would lose whatever sanity he had left.

The first change he made was going to the gym after his shift instead of straight home. He used to enjoy looking good and was a regular gym-goer in his past life in Kenya. He chose a small male-only gym and enjoyed working out and building muscle with like-minded people.

Once after his workout, one of the personal trainers invited him to come out for a drink. Kamal hesitated; he was expected home after all, but what the hell, he would go for one drink.

They went to the pub across the street from the gym. 'What can I get you, mate?' asked Bale.

'Whatever you're having,' he said. He watched his new friend walk up to the counter and observed him quietly. He was short and muscular but good-looking with a nice black sheen to his complexion. Kamal could tell he was African but didn't quite know which country he came from. He would have to ask him.

Bale came back with two beers and packets of crisps.

'Thanks, next round's on me. So, tell me, where are you from, man?'

What Will Be

'I'm originally from Uganda but have lived here for many years. You? India, Pakistan?'

'I'm from Kenya.'

'No way, man, you're a fellow East African!'

They spent a couple of happy hours just chatting and getting to know each other.

'I've got to go now but let's do this again. It's been fun,' Kamal said and got up to leave. He went to the toilet, rinsed his mouth out, hopped into his taxi, took out his mouth freshener spray from the glove compartment, and sprayed inside his mouth. For good measure, he also popped a mint in his mouth. It would not do for his in-laws to smell beer on him, although he was pretty sure they'd be in bed by the time he got back.

He got into the routine of going for a drink after the gym with Bale, and one day Bale said he was having a party and would Kamal come?

'Sure, I'd love to; I can't remember the last time I went to a proper party.'

On the night of the party, his wife noticed how handsome he looked and complimented him. 'Kamal, maybe we can try again tonight for a baby,' she said. She still hadn't become pregnant despite both of them trying very hard.

'Actually, I can't tonight; I have a party to go to.'

'What, whose, where, and how come you're not taking me?'

'I can't take you because I think it will be just the boys, you know, the ones from the gym.'

'Oh, OK, then, have fun.' Kulsum was disappointed; she hardly saw him as it was, what with him working all hours God sent and spending whatever spare time he had in the gym. She had long ago given up on her lover Afzal. She realised he would never leave his wife, so she decided to concentrate on her own marriage. In any case she felt she owed Kamal; he hadn't outed her after the wedding night when he had discovered she wasn't a virgin.

He saw the sad look she gave him and said, 'Don't worry, we'll try for the baby tomorrow night.'

He wasn't strictly honest with Kulsum; he had no idea what the party was; he had only made up the male-only bit just because he really didn't want her to come with him and meet his new friend Bale.

What Will Be

The flat was in Belgrave, an area populated by ethnic minorities, from the Asians who were kicked out of Uganda by the dictator Idi Amin to the more recent arrivals like the Somalis and Iraqi Kurds. He took the lift to the 9th floor of the tower block and knocked on Flat 10.

Bale answered the door and smiled warmly when he saw Kamal. 'Come in, bro, party's just starting. I'll get you a drink, then introduce you to everyone.' African music was blaring loudly from the sitting room. Several people sat around talking or dancing in the small space that spilt out to a tiny veranda. 'Hey, everyone, meet my friend Kamal! Kamal, meet everyone,' he laughed as he went to the kitchen to get drinks.

Kamal said 'hi' to everyone and someone made a space for him on the sofa. He sat down and surveyed his friend's pad. He had African paintings and masks everywhere, and a big clock shaped like the map of Uganda dominated a small wall. The party crowd was ethnically mixed, white, and black, but Kamal noticed that the men outnumbered the women. He also noticed two men gyrating against each other, and he looked away, feeling very uncomfortable.

Bale walked over to him and handed him a cold beer. 'Get that down you bro, you have a lot of catching up to do!'

Kamal accepted the beer with a smile.

'Help yourself to crisps, nuts, whatever, on the table next to you, man.'

'Thanks, I will.'

The beer flowed freely, and the music blasted from the two speakers strategically placed around the room. 'So, which one of these girls is your girlfriend?' he asked his friend.

'None of them bro, they're fag hags.'

'What?'

'Fag hags, just normal women who like hanging around gay men. I bat for the other team myself bro, hope that's not a problem?'

'Oh, no, not at all; I had many gay friends in Kenya.' It was true, he did have gay friends in Kenya, and although he had enjoyed their company and even almost got intimate once, he did not consider himself gay.

In his religion, being gay was the ultimate sin, punishable by death on earth and hellfire in the afterlife. He had put that shameful episode behind him, but now, his mind dulled by drink, he felt it resurface. He looked at

Bale and noticed how handsome he was as one of the white men sidled up to him and hugged him.

'Introduce me to your new friend properly, man. He's cute!'

'Back off, Jack, Kamal is not gay,' Bale said, pushing him away.

'You could have fooled me. He's been devouring you with his eyes all evening!'

'Go and annoy somebody else, Jack,' and Jack sashayed away with a wink and a knowing smile. 'Idiot, don't mind him,' Bale said as he sat down beside Kamal. 'He's had far too much to drink and a little something extra, no doubt.'

'No, it's OK, maybe he's right.'

It was Bale's turn to be astonished. 'What are you saying, bro?'

'Maybe I was looking at you; you are a good-looking man.' The drunker Kamal got, the better looking his friend became. 'You know I nearly went for a gay friend of mine once; he was joking, trying to wind me up and pressed himself against me. To my absolute horror, I realised I liked it. I don't know why I'm telling you this; I've never told this to a single soul.'

'No shame in that bro, you can't help who you fancy.'

'I guess not,' Kamal smiled as he accepted another beer from someone.

The party got more raucous as Kamal got drunker. In the end, he was up and dancing with the other guests, both male and female. Bale came to reclaim his friend, and Kamal danced with him when suddenly he kissed him.

Heart thumping, Kamal returned the kiss.

Jack, who noticed this, smiled mischievously, and said, 'Told ya he was gay!'

At this, Kamal recoiled, but Bale held him closer. 'It's OK, bro, let's go to my room,' and he silently led Kamal to the bedroom.

Bale closed the door, and instantly the music and the voices became a muffled sound. The room was quite big, dominated by a double bed with a Leicester Football Club duvet cover. The African masks were also evident here, as were the bark cloth wall hangings that Bale had brought back from Kampala to remind him of home. Bale took two more beer cans out of a mini-fridge next to the bed and handed one to Kamal.

What Will Be

The only place to sit was on the bed, so Kamal sat down, opened his can, and took a big swig. Bale sat next to him and did the same. Their senses were heightened, both anxiously aware that something was going to happen.

Last-minute nerves got the better of Kamal, and he stood up abruptly. 'I really shouldn't be doing this; I've got to go.'

'Relax, man, it's what you've always wanted, isn't it?' Bale said as he clamped his mouth on Kamal's and pushed him firmly onto the bed.

Kamal lost all sense of time, and when he woke up afterwards, he was stone-cold sober. He looked at the sleeping Bale, quickly gathered his clothes up, dressed and slipped out of the room. There were fewer people in the sitting room now, just the last few hagglers determined to party till dawn. He didn't look at anyone when he left, although he could feel the stares, the 'I know what you did' ones that bore into him even though he wasn't looking. It was long past midnight when the taxi dropped him off at home.

He quietly let himself in and prayed his mother-in-law wasn't in the kitchen for one of her midnight snacks or endless cups of tea. Thankfully she wasn't, and he crept up the stairs in the dark and tiptoed to his bedroom. Again, he prayed Kulsum wasn't awake, but she was snoring gently. He desperately needed a shower, but he would wake everyone up as there was only the one bathroom, and that was next to his in-law's bedroom. So, he slipped into bed beside his wife, but could not sleep, the night's event going over and over again in his mind. He had slept with a man.

Oh my God! He was gay, or was he? He felt disgusted with himself and at the same time excited. What was wrong with him? Was he always like this? Was this what he always wanted, as Bale had told him? 'I'm going to burn in hell for this,' he told himself over and over again as the guilt and shame over what he had done clawed deeper and deeper into him.

'Oh God, please help me,' he prayed silently into the night. He knew there would be no help from God; as a Muslim male, he had committed the ultimate sin, not only unforgivable but one that would damn him to hellfire for all eternity.

At daybreak, he would read the Quran and remind himself of what it says about homosexuality and start begging for forgiveness. He hated him-

What Will Be

self, he smelt of Bale, but he couldn't wash him off. He curled into a ball and silently wept till eventually, he fell asleep in the early hours.

When he woke up, his first thought was the shower; he had to get clean. He felt dirty, sleazy, and wept again as the hot water cascaded deliciously down his back. 'Please wash my sin away,' he prayed as he scrubbed himself raw with his wife's loofah.

Chapter 22

London

The recruitment agency began to bore Ayan, and she started looking for other jobs. A friend mentioned that with her command of languages, she should try interpreting. She applied to a few agencies but then got the ideal job as a Somali interpreter in the Home Office. This job was both varied and interesting. She was glad it was the Home Office she was working for and not one of the many translation agencies that had sprung up all over the UK. She had heard of one agency started by a Russian woman who exploited her interpreters and translators. This woman was either a clever businesswoman or a crook depending on how you were brought up; she paid the interpreters pittance and charged her clients a fortune for their services. She had made enough money to buy a villa in Portugal. To gain and keep major contracts like the police or the solicitors, she would bribe them by offering her villa free of charge. Apparently, she had a degree in psychology or psychiatry which she also used to good effect. She would flatter both her interpreters and clients in her heavily accented English, 'but you look beautiful today!' even if they didn't.

To keep her interpreters sweet, she would offer help and go as far as loaning money to any of them. Ayan cracked up when she heard this story. 'And I thought corruption only occurred in Africa'! 'No, it's alive and well in the UK as well dear sister!'

She enjoyed the work; it was varied and interesting. However, she couldn't get over the naiveté and ignorance of the immigration officers and the solicitors while interviewing people.

As an interpreter, she had to abide by the industry's code of conduct. Confidentiality was crucial, so she could not even talk to her friends about her daily work nor tell the officers or solicitors when someone was clearly lying. She was, above all, being paid to be a mouthpiece and not to offer her advice or opinion. She sat on cases where the person said they were Somali but did not look or speak, much less understand the language. In one such incident, the interviewee was asked what other language he spoke, and he replied that he spoke Swahili. Ayan was asked if she spoke this language, and of course, she did, having spent time in Kenya. So, she ended up in-

What Will Be

terpreting for a Kenyan man who convinced the authorities, if not her, that he was Somali, from the Juba region, and that because he was Bantu, was being persecuted by the Somalis. The officers accepted this and granted him asylum.

Ayan was incensed, but she could do nothing; the Kenyan knew this and gave her a smirk. She told him point-blank, 'I know you're not Somali.'

The officer, quickly interjecting, asked, 'What was that?'

'Oh nothing, I was just letting him know the interview is over.'

She told her friends about this story when she went home, and they couldn't believe it either.

'You mean the immigration guy couldn't see the difference between you and the Kenyan?' Yasmin asked.

'Oh, but black people all look the same,' Amal said, laughing. 'Forget about it, Ayan, let them let in whoever they want into their country. You can't police them all. The other day in the cinema when I went to buy popcorn, I noticed the cashier's name was Fartun. Nice name, I said. Where are you from? 'Somalia,' she told me without any embarrassment. I mean, she could see I was Somali, and I could certainly see she one hundred percent wasn't remotely Somali! So, there you go, Ayan, everyone who wants to come to the UK only has to say they are Somali and they're in!'

'The British are way too tolerant, and to cap it all, they are so naive that they believe whatever they are told. They feel so sorry for these 'poor' asylum seekers seeking refuge and safety in their country. They just have no way of comprehending that some of these 'poor' people are actually richer than they are and can speak perfect English as well as several other languages.'

Sometimes she was astounded by the ignorance of the interviewing officer. 'Somalia, is that North Africa? How did you get to this country?' Obviously not by camel, Ayan thought often but, out loud said, 'Uh, they took a flight, and Somalia is in East Africa.' She resented educating them, but she felt she had to. She always wondered how these people could do a job where they knew so little about world geography, people, and cultures.

Before she joined the home office, she had been asked to do some freelance interpreting for Somali people.

What Will Be

The first thing she noticed was that Somalis were losing their culture and identity. The women spoke to their children in English, and when she asked them why, the answer was always, 'Because English is better, what use is Somali?' These answers usually came from mothers who could barely speak English themselves.

Whenever she heard this, Ayan suppressed a smile. She knew that they insisted on their children speaking English so that they could learn the language from them instead of going to school themselves. Also, because the mothers were not educated, they had little knowledge of just how valuable a mother tongue was. She would often advise the women to 'Please speak to your children in Somali; it's really important. If a society loses its language, it has nothing. Language is what sets us apart and identifies us as a people. Otherwise, your children will be classified as Black British in a few years, no different from other Africans and the Afro-Caribbean community. If you lose your language, you lose everything.' Of course, all this fell on deaf ears, and the mothers carried on thinking that it was 'civilised' to speak English only with their children.

The other thing she noticed was the growing lack of respect between young people and their elders. Throughout her life, she was taught to respect her elders. Elders were not just parents and grandparents; it included anyone older than you, like older siblings. She now had cases where children as young as eleven were reporting their parents to the police because they weren't allowed to play football or go out with their friends. The breakdown of families was also hard to digest, such as the single mother who spent her benefits on qat and cigarettes. She would chew qat all night and would not get her children up and ready for school. The outcome being that the children dressed themselves and went to school all by themselves. The school would eventually notice that the children were hungry and dishevelled and would notify Social Services, who would put in a call of child neglect. The children would be fostered, leaving the mother weeping, and wondering where it all went wrong.

Ayan told her friends some of these stories whenever they met up for one of their many long lunches. This weekend it was the turn of Bilan to host and they were all full and satisfied from the wonderful spread she had put together.

'Anyway, friends, I have to go now. Zumba calls!' Ayan said.

What Will Be

'Waste of time,' said one of her friends. 'Do you keep your hijab on?'

'Of course, I do; I used to get strange looks at first, but now no one really notices, and we just get in the groove, as they used to say! Although once in a lift at the hospital, a man looked me up and down and said, 'It's good you're dressed like that.'

'Like what? I asked.'

'Western.' I thought about asking him what was good about that but thought better of it. No point arguing with an ignoramus.'

Ayan really enjoyed her Zumba classes; the teacher was very good and had the best Latin dance music ever. Her sister Amina and some friends couldn't understand how she could dance sexily and suggestively, without abandon and still go to the mosque and pray. 'I can do both, and anyway, my class is exclusively female, it's not as if I'm dancing with men, so what's the harm? I have a friend who refuses to do a female-only self-defence class because she says you're more likely to be attacked by a man than a woman. If a woman attacks her, at least they'll be on equal footing!'

Southampton

Most weekends, Ayan travelled by coach to Southampton. She used the two and a half hours travel time from Victoria Station to read books and study the Quran. She loved going there to see both Amina and Anab. This weekend was no exception; Amina collected her from the Central Bus Station and drove home with her. 'It's so green here; I love it,' she said to her sister. 'Where I live in London, I don't see trees or greenery.'

'But you said Southampton was boring!'

'That's before I got used to living in the concrete jungle.'

'Then move here; there are five parks in the city,' Amina said.

'No, too boring. I like the bright lights of the city!' Laughing, they went up the lift to Amina's floor, and as soon as Amina opened the door, Ayan flung herself into Anab's arms. 'Mum! I've missed you!'

Anab held her tight and kissed both her cheeks. 'How are you, my daughter? Have you lost weight?'

'Only a little Mum, you know I go dancing.'

'Dancing, shmanzing, you don't need it. Who's going to marry you if you get too skinny?'

'It's OK, Mum, I've only lost a little and anyway, in this country, men don't like fat women.'

'But our men love fat women; they think a beautiful woman is a fat, fair one.'

'Who says I'm going to marry a Somali man?'

'Oh, oh, maybe she has an English boyfriend,' Amina teased her sister.

'No, I don't! I have no time for boyfriends, and anyway, I would never marry a non-Muslim, so that rules out most Englishmen.'

Amina knew that was a dig at her, but she chose to ignore it.

Over dinner, she told them about her work and her life in London. 'Mum, talking about Somali men and fat women, I had a funny case once. It wasn't strictly interpreting or translating, rather explaining cultural nuances to someone. An English lady who manages a block of flats had complained that every time she entered the lift if there were Somali men present, they either left immediately or put as much distance as possible between her and them. 'Why? Is it because I'm fat or because I'm white?' she asked me. 'Trust me, it's not. It's because they've done their ablutions and are ready for prayer, so no contact with women. Besides, Somali men love fat women; they'd love you also because you're fair. They don't like me because I'm too thin and too dark! I can tell you that made her day.'

'Crisis averted!' Amina laughed as she planned their weekend ahead. She was happy, her agency was doing well and winning awards, her sister was happy and healthy, her mum content and her relationship with Dylan went from strength to strength.

Leicester

'What time did you get home last night? I couldn't wait any longer for you and went to bed.'

Kamal looked at Kulsum and said, 'Oh, around midnight, I think it was. The party was pretty boring.' A tight smile played on Kulsum's lips.

'Fucking liar!' she thought. She knew he had come in at five in the morning, she had pretended to be asleep, and when he got into bed with her, he stank to high heaven. She had to stop herself from gagging. She had given up Afzal for him, was even beginning to love him, to want to have his

What Will Be

babies, and this was how he repaid her. By sleeping with another woman. Well, the baby plans will be put on hold immediately. She would go to her GP and get back on the pill. Of course, she couldn't tell her parents what was happening. It was too shameful; besides, she still felt that she owed Kamal.

Over the next few days, she noticed the change in him. He started reading the Quran daily, and he had started going to the mosque again for prayers. He stopped going to the gym.

Her parents were pleased, 'Masha Allah, what a good man he is. You're lucky to have him as your husband, Kulsum.'

'Yeah, right,' she thought, 'if only you knew what he had done.'

Every time he went down on his knees, he asked God, with tears in his eyes, for forgiveness, but driving his taxi around the cold, dark streets of Leicester at night, his mind would wander to 'that night' and how he felt. He'd never felt like that with Amina, Kulsum or any of his numerous former girlfriends.

He came home deliberately late; he knew he couldn't make good his promise to try for a baby. Because he was so occupied with his guilt and longing for Bale, he failed to notice that Kulsum barely looked or spoke to him. Soon lust overcame prayer, and he went back to the gym in search of Bale. He found him in the weights section surrounded by admiring males. He had the physique of someone who spent his life in the gym, his bulging biceps shown off to great advantage in a white, sleeveless vest. His dark skin glistened with sweat, and his face broke into a smile as he saw Kamal. He dropped his barbell and walked towards him. 'Hey, man, where've you been? Haven't seen you since the party.'

Kamal smiled uncomfortably. 'Oh, been busy, man. You know how it is, with work and family.'

Bale looked him up and down. 'Come on then, let's get that body working.'

Kamal was not a gym rat; he only went because he hadn't wanted to go home to Kulsum and her parents every night and sit in front of the TV watching Bollywood films. He never really did weights until he met Bale; he was more of a cardio man, which meant running on the treadmill. That's how he had retained his skinny frame, but now watching Bale, he wanted to be like him; he wanted to bulk up and have a six-pack. So, he tried to copy him in whatever he was doing during the workout. Still, he couldn't manage the heavier weights, so he gave up, sweating and panting heavily after a while.

'Man, you can't go full steam,' Bale told him. 'You need to build up over time; Rome wasn't built in a day! I'm all done in; fancy a drink later? I'll just go shower and change.'

It was the start of Kamal's forage into homosexuality. Bale introduced him to gay clubs and gay culture, and he proved to be a willing and eager student. He got little comfort when one of his new friends told him that it seemed he also liked women. He was not gay but bisexual. He had never even considered the thought that he might be bisexual until then.

Kulsum kept observing the change in him; he still went to the mosque for prayers but spent one or two nights a week away from home, always with a new excuse.

'My company is sending me to London,' was one she thought particularly funny. What taxi firm sends its drivers to London and for what? Another was, 'A friend has arrived from Kenya, and I have to go see him.' She also noticed that he used her tweezers to pluck his eyebrows and used her perfumes when he thought she wasn't looking. Something fishy was definitely going on, and she was going to find out, whatever that was.

Chapter 23

Southampton

Dylan had proposed to Amina. With his business growing day by day, he felt that the time was right for him to get married and start a family. Amina had accepted, of course, but with the proviso that he convert to Islam. She told him she couldn't possibly marry him as a Christian. He immediately agreed by joking that giving up pork and alcohol was a small price to pay for having her as his wife.

'Of course, you'll also have to pay dowry,' she informed him.

'What's that?'

'My bride price! In Somali culture, you have to pay my family the bride price, in cash or gold, to be distributed to family members. It's to thank the family for bringing up the woman you're going to marry, you're lucky, in the old days it used to be camels. A hundred camels, a family's entire wealth! Luckily for you, I have no family except Ayan and Anab.'

He had taken Amina to his parent's home to break the news to them. After dinner, he told his parents that he and Amina were engaged. The mother almost choked on her over boiled broccoli, while the father jumped out of his chair, gave Amina a hug with the words, 'Grandchildren, yes!' He congratulated his son as his wife sat stony-faced and said nothing.

Dylan was too happy to notice his mother's reaction. Still, Amina knew trouble lay ahead between her and the mother of the man she loved, just as she'd known during their first meeting.

Ayan was pleased Dylan would convert; she would have a brother, at last, something she always wanted. It took a bit of time to convince Anab. Of course, she wanted Amina to get married, but she wanted her to marry a nice Somali boy. 'I love Dylan, Mum, it's that simple.'

'Love, what's that? I had an arranged marriage to Yusuf, and we were together for many years until God took him. I respected him and cared for him throughout his life. He never complained once, not even when I couldn't give him children.

'Well, I want to marry Dylan, so please give me your blessing.'

What Will Be

'You'll always have my blessing, my daughter. But we have a problem, who's going to give you away? You have no male relatives.'

'I hadn't thought of that. Can't you give me away?'

'No, of course not; it has to be a male relative!'

'I don't have one, so let's leave it for now.'

Ayan had also met someone, a Somali lawyer who she met through her interpreting work. Omar was born in London, but his family came from Mogadishu, so, as she always teased him, he was 'Fish and Chips', the term used for British born Somalis.

Amina had met him and liked him instantly, and she knew he would make Ayan happy. He had proposed long before Dylan, but according to Somali culture, the eldest child had to get married first, so Ayan would have to wait a little longer.

London

The following weekend, Amina and Anab went to London to see Ayan and also to buy her wedding dress. Ayan was taking them to Southall, where numerous Somali-owned shops pretty much sold the same things. The shops were actually little units next to each other, mainly owned and staffed by women. Competition for customers was high, so each time they passed a unit, the shopkeeper would entice them with either a discount if they shopped there or tea and biscuits.

Amina found a beautiful bridal dhirac, the Somali kaftan, in red with gold thread woven through it. It shimmered brightly when it caught the light. The shopkeeper convinced her to team it with gold, high heeled sandals. She also found the traditional Somali guntino that brides of old used to wear but was now making a comeback with modern Somali brides. She then found the traditional yellow amber beads that went with the outfit. She bought herself a gold set comprising of necklace, earrings and bangles that traditionally would have been given to her by her mother.

Anab felt bad knowing that she couldn't buy what Amina needed, but she didn't expect Anab to buy anything; she was a refugee and had no money. Besides, it was her turn to look after Anab now.

Southampton

What Will Be

The nikah would take place in Southampton, but there would be no wedding party because the family did not know enough people in the city. Dylan had many friends but no close family other than his parents, so he didn't mind that there were no big wedding plans; he just wanted to marry Amina and start his new life with her. Amina and Anab were both going to move in with him; he had plenty of space for both.

His mother tried to discourage him, 'It's one thing to have a new wife in the house, but to have her mother as well? That's not a good idea.'

Dylan explained as patiently as he could that Anab was welcome in his house. It was what his fiancée wanted, and because he loved her, it was what he wanted too. He also explained to his mother that if it wasn't for Anab, both Amina and Ayan would probably not even be alive.

Amina had told him that Anab was reluctant to move in with them; she had thought that her new husband wouldn't want an old Somali woman in his house and that she could always go to London and live with Ayan. Amina persuaded her to stay in Southampton; she explained to her that Ayan was busy all the time and she would be very lonely sitting in a flat by herself all day. 'At least here, you have your friends and both of us. And if anything happens or you need me, I'm not too far away and can home quickly. Ali will also come for you every day as he's been doing, so nothing will change really, except we'll be in a new environment.'

Ali, the Somali taxi driver, turned out to be a good friend to Amina and Anab. They enlisted his help for the nikah; he went to see the Imam at the mosque and secured a date for them. He knew Amina had no living male relatives, and he offered to step in and give her away. He would also bring one of his friends to be a witness.

Anab asked one of the young women she made friends with at Mayran's to do Amina's henna which would be elaborate for the wedding. 'You should have a proper Somali wedding after the nikah at the mosque, auntie,' one of the women said to her.

'Amina doesn't want that; she wants a simple affair.'

'But she'll miss all the fun of a Somali wedding, the traditional dances, the poetry, the gifts, the praising of the bride and groom and their families, all that.'

'Never mind, I'm just happy she's getting married and, to a good man.'

What Will Be

Ayan had come down to Southampton for her sister's nikah, arranged for a Saturday to accommodate all working parties.

On the day, Amina, Ayan and Anab got up early. They had breakfast shortly after which Ali brought the young woman Sagal who was to do her henna.

Sagal, a fat chatty woman, was also an amateur beautician and hairdresser who was always in demand at Somali weddings in the city. She quickly drew beautiful designs on both Amina's hands, up to her elbows and then her feet up to mid-calf. 'Let me do your makeup too, Amina, nothing too much as you're going to the mosque, but if you can't look beautiful on your wedding day, when can you?'

Amina complied and even allowed Sagal to put qasil, the herbal face mask Somali women swore by, on her face. She sat with a green face while Ayan and Anab kept themselves busy perfuming Amina's wedding dhirac with unsi, the scent that identified Somali women and made them stand out in every crowd. Every family had a secret ingredient for their fragrance, including which pure perfume oil they used, but the result was always the same, lovely, and intoxicating albeit sometimes a little too overpowering. A tiny amount put on the burner would perfume the whole house.

Dylan rang her, and they chatted for a bit while she waited for both the henna and the qasil to dry on her face. 'Can't wait to see you later this evening, and I still can't believe we'll be married by tonight.'

'Me too, although if you see me now, you might change your mind!'

'Never, but why?'

'Well, my hair is in rollers, my face is covered in green gunk, my hands and feet are orange etc. etc.!'

'I'm sure you still look beautiful, darling!' he laughed.

When he hung up, Sagal asked if that was the groom, and Amina replied that it was. Sagal happened to be a great gossip, and Amina knew that all the Somalis in Southampton would hear about the Somali girl marrying a white man by the time she left her flat. Somalis were very proud of their ancestry and did not encourage marriages with outsiders. The only ones looked on favourably were the Arabs because of cultural and religious reasons. Some Somalis had Arab blood in them. Usually, Somali women sometimes married outside their own, but this wasn't the case for Somali men because they preferred their own women who they considered the most beautiful and cleanest in the world. Things were slowly changing with the diaspora, though, and more and more men were now getting married to foreign women.

Ali came promptly at six to collect them, and they drove through the city to the mosque where Dylan was waiting with his parents. As instructed, the mother had a scarf covering her hair and a long skirt on as well as a disapproving look. The father also had on an orange headscarf until Ali asked him to take it off. Men didn't need to cover their hair. In any case, the orange scarf was a Sikh covering, not a Muslim one!

Inside the mosque, the Imam welcomed them and asked them to sit on the floor which was covered with beautiful carpets. The Imam had the Quran open before him, 'Which couple is getting married and I believe we have one coming to our religion, praise be to Allah.'

Ali introduced everyone to the Imam, who said the conversion had to be done first before the marriage. He motioned Dylan to come forward. 'Have you chosen a Muslim name, or should we give you one?'

'You can give me one, sir; I don't know any.'

'Very well, what religion do you follow now?'

'Well, I'm Church of England, but I don't really follow it.'

'So, you're Christian. A people of the book, but do you understand that you will have to renounce your religion to become a Muslim?'

'Yes, sir, I do.'

'And do you understand anything of our religion, what it entails, what is required of you?'

'Yes, Amina has told me a lot about it and given me some literature as well as a copy of the Quran in English which I have started reading.'

'Excellent start! It's very easy to convert to Islam, but to follow it properly is very difficult, but you're on the right track. Let's begin. All you have to do is take the Shahadah or Testimony, a declaration of your new faith. So, repeat after me in Arabic, but first I better tell you what you will be repeating. There is no God but Allah, and Mohammad is the messenger of Allah.'

Dylan repeated the unfamiliar words, and then the Imam bestowed the name Daniyal on him; it was closer to his own name but had the honour of being a prophet's name and meaning intelligent or intellectual. Dylan was pleased with that.

'Today, your past sins have been washed away; it's as if you are a newborn. Welcome to Islam, you are our son and brother now. Embrace your new community.'

Ali and his witness friend embraced him, and the Imam said, 'Now, to the other important matter. Step forward the bride.'

Amina moved and sat beside Dylan. The Imam asked her if she wanted to marry this man, and she answered in the affirmative. He read the relevant verse from the Quran. He asked the couple to exchange vows before their witnesses, Dylan's being Ali and his friend and Amina's Ayan and Anab.

The Imam then produced a Nikah or marriage contract and asked them both to sign it, then passed it over to the witnesses to sign as well. When this was done, the Imam congratulated them, gave blessings, and wished them a long, happy marriage.

Anab shed a few tears of happiness as she finally embraced her new son-in-law. Being more forgiving and open-minded than his wife, Dylan's father was overjoyed; he'd enjoyed the ceremony even though there were a few things he didn't understand. The mother finally came over to Amina and her family and offered her congratulations. Amina was her daughter-in-law now, whether she liked it or not.

Outside the mosque, Amina thanked Ali and his friend for being her husband's witnesses and for him standing in as her male relative. Dylan's parents said their goodbyes and left. She started walking towards Ali's car, and Anab stopped her. 'Where are you going? Ali is taking us home, not you. You go with your husband now. We'll see you next week; in the meantime, Ayan will help me get packed ready to move in with you.'

Amina got in Dylan's car. It felt strange not to be going home with her family, but she also felt happy that she was going home, her home together with her new husband. Both being busy with their businesses, they had no time for a honeymoon. However, Dylan promised his new wife that he would take her anywhere in the world she wanted at a later date. Exactly a week later, Anab moved in, and Ayan returned to London.

Chapter 24

Leicester

Kamal's in-laws were getting more and more frustrated with him. They had expected the young couple to have had at least two children by now, but none were forthcoming. They hardly saw him as it was, and when they did, he was always in a hurry to go somewhere.

Kulsum couldn't tell her parents that Kamal hadn't touched her in a year, although initially, he had made an effort. He only slept with her out of duty and hoped she would get pregnant to occupy herself with a child and not with him. Kulsum couldn't get pregnant, and Kamal took that to mean God was punishing him for asking Amina to abort their child. Through his boyfriend Bale, he had met other gay men, men he thought understood him and never judged him, and he moved further and further away from his family, his community, and his religion.

On a bright Saturday afternoon one summer, Kulsum, who had been out grocery shopping, passed by the gym that Kamal frequented. She decided to she would surprise him and ask him if he wanted to have a coffee with her. She climbed up the stairs to the gym and spotted him immediately, but to her utter amazement, a black guy was caressing him even as he showed him how to lift the barbell.

Kamal sensed her presence and quickly moved away from Bale when he saw his wife. Bale grabbed his hand and pulled him back, saying 'Where you going darling?' as he followed Kamal towards Kulsum.

'Darling? What the hell is going on?' Kulsum demanded to know.

Embarrassed and furious with Bale, Kamal said, 'Nothing is going on, and what are you doing here anyway?'

'I came to ask if you wanted to go for coffee, but I see you are otherwise engaged. Now I understand, this man is your lover.'

'You don't understand anything; go wait outside for me.'

'No, I'm not waiting, you can deny it as much as you like, but I know what you are now, a filthy, cheating, lying shit!' She stormed out, and Bale put a hand out to him, but Kamal brushed it off.

What Will Be

'Back off, man. I'm ruined, if she tells her parents, they'll tell my parents, and soon, the communities in both Nairobi and Leicester will know. I'll be ostracised, finished, my life is over.' Kamal ran out of the gym onto the street outside and caught up with Kulsum. 'Kulsum, please wait a minute.', he pleaded.

'Get away from me!'

He had to stop her blabbing to her parents somehow. 'Listen to me, Kulsum. That man calls everyone darling.'

'Yeah, but he was very pally and touchy-feely with you.'

'Honestly, he's like that with everyone; it's just the way he is.'

'I'm just going to come out and ask you straight, Kamal. Are you gay?'

He laughed nervously, unconvincingly. 'Me, gay? No way, besides, I'm married to you.'

'That doesn't stop anyone. My friends and I know of a couple of Pakistani married men with children who are gay.'

'Well, I'm not, OK?'

'OK, if you say so, but something doesn't feel right.' To keep her sweet, he said he was planning to take her for dinner that night anyway, just the two of them. She calmed down and agreed that dinner would be a good idea.

He was extra nice to her that evening, complimenting her on her outfit and making her laugh with some new jokes. He had to make sure she was firmly on his side and would not tell anyone about what she witnessed at the gym. She noticed that he seemed more relaxed, just like the old Kamal. 'Try my saag paneer,' he said as he held a spoonful to her mouth. 'You are beautiful, you know. Thanks for being my wife and being so sweet.' Kulsum, who wasn't used to his compliments, lapped them up now.

She still had her suspicions, but she decided to give him the benefit of the doubt and ignore her suspicion.

The next day, he went to see Bale at his flat. 'Sorry about yesterday, man. I don't know what she was thinking coming to the gym.'

'I don't know what you're doing here, man. Go home to your wife.'

'But I want to be here with you.'

What Will Be

Bale turned to him cold and furious. 'I left Uganda because they would kill me if they found out I was gay. This is the UK, man, you can be free to express your sexuality, and you don't have to be afraid.'

'I just can't; you'll never understand.'

'OK then, let's call it a day. I can't be with someone who leads a double life and can't be true to themselves.'

Kamal disgusted himself even further by begging Bale. 'Please don't do this. I love you, I don't love my wife, and I already told you our marriage was arranged.'

Bale stood firm. 'I have no time for this man. Call me when you sort yourself out. Now get out!'

Kamal left the flat, took the stairs instead of the lift, sat on a step and cried miserably. Why was this happening to him? Why couldn't he control himself? After a few minutes, he stood up, walked down the stairs to his taxi and out of Bale's life. He decided he would try to be a good husband to his wife and forget about men.

Kulsum was happy she was now getting all his attention, there were no more trips to London, and he came home every evening. A sense of calm and peace descended on the house; everyone seemed happier. Kamal wanted to try for a baby again and even helped his wife more around the house.

Kulsum still had her suspicions, but now a baby mattered more to her than Kamal. Months passed without incident in the household.

Kulsum's mother teased her, 'You've put on weight; what is he feeding you, my daughter?'

She hadn't thought anyone would notice her weight gain. It was true she was eating more and craving Twix chocolates all the time. She had taken to buying them in bulk and snacking on them whenever the craving hit her, which was several times a day.

She was having tea with her mother in the kitchen one day when she suddenly ran to the bathroom and threw up. Her mother heard and realised the true reason for her daughter's weight gain.

When she came back to the kitchen, a very happy, excited mother told her, 'I think you're pregnant, Kulsum.'

Kulsum sat down for a moment, absorbed the news, and promptly burst into tears.

What Will Be

Her mother was alarmed. 'What's the matter, child? I thought you'd be happy. You've waited long enough.'

'I am happy mum; these are tears of happiness because I just thought it would never happen to me. I have suspected that I might be pregnant, but I dismissed the idea.'

'First, we have to make an appointment with the doctor; I'm going to do it now,' said he excited mother. 'Second, we'll break the happy news to your dad and your husband.' Mother and daughter hugged each other tightly.

When everyone was home, they had dinner as usual and then went to the sitting room with their tea. 'Well?' said the father.

'Well, what?' said the mother.

'I know you are itching to tell us something, so get on with it!'

'How do you know I have something to say? Are you a wizard or something?'

'I have been married to you for forty years, and I know when you're dying to say something. Go on, tell us the latest gossip from your women's sewing group.'

'OK, then, the latest from my women's sewing group is that you're going to be a grandfather.'

'What?' the cry came from both Kamal and his father-in-law.

'Kulsum is pregnant; I've made an appointment with the doctor for tomorrow.'

Both the father and Kamal jumped up to hug Kulsum. 'At last, God has blessed us, Nazia; we are going to be grandparents.'

Kamal was ecstatic, too; he loved children and had always envied some of his friends who had children. That night he held Kulsum close, and she realised it was the closest they'd ever been in their entire married life. 'Mohamed if it's a boy, and Medina if it's a girl,' he told his wife.

'What, I have no choice in the naming? I don't like Medina; if it's a girl, I want her to be named after my mum, Nazia.'

Kamal laughed happily. 'Look at us, arguing about a name for a child who isn't even born. Tell you what, let's wait till the baby is actually here.'

What Will Be

At ten the next morning, the happy quartet made their way to the hospital. After a short wait, they were called in. The doctor examined Kulsum, told her she was indeed pregnant then asked her to lift her top up to take an ultrasound to find out how many weeks the foetus was. As the excited family hovered round, the doctor ran the wand over Kulsum's stomach, hummed and aahed, and did it again until Kamal asked if everything was alright.

'More than alright. Congratulations, you're having twins!'

Whoops erupted all-around, more tears of joy from the prospective parents and grandparents.

'Thank you, doctor, thank you so much,'

Kulsum's father was almost bowing to the doctor as though he personally was responsible for the miracle.

The doctor prescribed the necessary vitamins and other supplements and made an appointment to see the expectant mother in six weeks.

They went to the best Punjabi restaurant in Leicester to celebrate, after which the father took them all to the mosque to give thanks to God for the blessing they had been bestowed with.

Amidst this happiness and goodwill, Kamal's thoughts went briefly to Amina and the baby he made her abort. He wondered whether it was a boy or a girl; he wondered if she had children of her own.

Six weeks later, Kulsum woke up in the middle of the night with cramping stomach pains. She made her way slowly and quietly to the bathroom. She didn't want to wake Kamal, who was snoring heavily but was alarmed when she saw blood trickling down her legs and leaving a trail on the floor. She stepped into the shower to wash it off, then went to wake her husband. She shook him gently, calling his name until he opened his eyes and sat up abruptly.

'What's wrong?'

'I'm bleeding, and my stomach hurts. Something's wrong; we need to go to the hospital.'

He jumped quickly out of bed, pulled on a pair of tracksuit bottoms, and grabbed his car keys. 'Let's go.'

'What about Mama and Papa, shall I wake them up?'

'Do it quickly then.'

What Will Be

She knocked on her parent's door and told them they were going to the hospital because she wasn't feeling very well. 'Go back to bed; I just wanted to let you know in case you woke up and found us not here.'

'No, wait, we're coming with you. We can't sleep now anyway, knowing you're not well.' They dressed quickly, got in the car, and drove to the hospital.

There wasn't much traffic on the road at that time, so the journey was fairly short. Luckily, fewer people were at A&E, and because she was bleeding and pregnant, it was seen as a priority. The doctor who examined her was a gruff Egyptian who had never left the country again after getting his medical degree. This is what he hated about medicine, breaking bad news to people. 'I'm very sorry, you've had a miscarriage.'

'Miscarriage, what do you mean?' demanded Kulsum's mother.

'Sadly, the babies are no more.'

The family, inconsolable, were in tears, only this time, not of happiness, but of sorrow and the loss of not one, but two babies.

The doctor tried to be reassuring, but he wasn't sure if anyone was listening to him. 'You are a young couple. Insha'Allah, you will be blessed with many more children.'

In the weeks that followed, dark and miserable despair descended upon the house. It was as if the happiness had been sucked out of the home. Kulsum's parents retreated to their bedroom; they no longer sat on the comfortable sofa in the sitting room to watch Bollywood films. Kulsum also took to her bed and spent hours crying while Kamal watched helplessly. Nothing he could do or say would get her out of her depression. She told him this was a punishment from God for his homosexual tendencies. He denied it again, but she knew deep down that he was lying. As for him, the bottom had fallen out of his world. He was really looking forward to being a father, but he knew that he never would be. God had finally shown him his displeasure by taking away his twins. He regretted now more than ever making Amina get an abortion all those years ago. Why, oh, why did he do it? Now he understood her pain, why she hated him so much, and the suffering and anguish he had caused her. He should never have agreed to marry his cousin when his heart was with Amina. He had to get out of here.

On one of the rare occasions that his aunt and uncle came downstairs, he blurted out, 'I'm going home.'

What Will Be

They both looked at him in surprise. 'Home. Where? This is your home.'

'No, I mean home to Nairobi. I have to go before I lose my mind here. Kulsum can't bear to look at me, never mind talk to me, I never see you two. I miss my parents, my sister, my brother, I miss Nairobi.'

They could see he had made his mind up, and nothing they could say would change his mind. 'Maybe a holiday would do you good. Have you told Kulsum?'

'No, Auntie, the idea came to me just now. I'll go up and tell her.' He found her still in bed, awake but hugging her duvet. He called her name, but she turned her face away as soon as she heard his voice. 'I've decided to go back to Nairobi for a while just to give each of us the time and space to grieve.'

Slowly she turned to look at him, a look of pure hatred on her face. 'Go and don't bother coming back; I don't care. All this is your fault.'

He saw that it was useless arguing with her and so he left the house, went to the nearest travel agency, and booked his ticket to Nairobi.

Nazia went to check on her daughter, she was expecting to comfort her, but she found her strangely calm. 'Don't worry, my daughter, let him go; the break will do you both good, and when he comes back, you can try for another baby.'

'I don't want him to come back; I hate him.'

'It's the grief talking child. He's your husband; you don't really hate him.'

She did hate him, but how could she explain why to her mother, his aunt?

On a cold, misty Saturday morning, a taxi driver from his firm came to collect Kamal to take him to the bus stop where he was taking the bus to Heathrow Airport. His uncle and aunt hugged him goodbye and stood by the door as the taxi drove away. Kulsum heard her parents shut the front door, pulled her duvet over her, and went to sleep, peacefully and at last happily.

Chapter 25

Nairobi

After a nine-hour flight, Kamal landed at Jomo Kenyatta International Airport very early in the morning. Just before landing, he had looked out of the window, and saw the familiar sights, spotted the Ngong Hills, the Athi Plains and even a giraffe. He knew he was home as a heavyweight seemed to have been lifted from his shoulders.

As he stepped off the plane, he breathed in the fresh morning air and resisted the urge to kiss the ground like they did in films. All he had to do now was go through customs, and he would be out of the airport and in Nairobi for the first time in years. As a returning Kenyan, he cleared the visa section quickly, but customs was an entirely different kettle of fish.

A customs officer called him over. 'Jambo. Put your suitcase here. What have you got in there? What have you brought for us?'

Kamal laughed; he had forgotten the Kenyan mentality of always asking for 'a little something.'

'Just my clothes, bwana.'

'You're from England, land of the Queen. You sure you don't have presents in there?'

He did have presents for his family, but he wanted to get away; he hadn't slept very well on the plane. If the customs officer was going to let him go and not waste time opening his suitcase and rifling through his clothes, he would have to bribe him. Knowing they preferred hard currency to local, he produced ten pounds, slipped it into the man's waiting hands. With a smile, he was told to go on his way.

Outside the terminal, he scanned the waiting crowd to find his brother, who was collecting him. He saw Safraz waving frantically, and he smiled and waved back to his brother.

The brothers hugged each other, with Safraz teasing him. 'Look how skinny you are. Is there no food in England? Don't worry, Mum will soon fatten you up!'

They chatted all the way home as Kamal noticed that new buildings, either flats or offices, had been built on either side of Uhuru Highway.

What Will Be

'Progress, my friend!' joked Safraz. 'On a serious note, not that good, because the developers are slowly encroaching on the game park scaring the animals and spoiling the environment, but hey, this is Kenya. Who cares about anything but making money?'

Safraz hooted his horn when they arrived home, and the metal gate was opened by the Masai askari. His mother, father and sister, Maryam, rushed out of the house just as he rushed out of the car to envelop them in big hugs. His mother and his sister could not stop kissing him. His parents looked older but well.

The front of the house looked like it could do with a lick of paint; the paint cracked and faded. He resolved to hire some fundis to do it up in the next couple of days, but for now, he basked in his family's love and warmth.

His mother had prepared his favourite breakfast, parathas with aloo sabzhi, the spicy, tangy potato curry, mango pickle and masala chai. No one could make breakfast quite like his mother. He ate his breakfast, opened his suitcase, and gave them all their gifts from the UK, then had a shower and went to sleep for a few hours. He slept in his old bedroom, cleaned, and prepped for his visit and had the best sleep he had for a long time. He was home, happy, safe, and cocooned in love.

Kamal spent the next few weeks catching up with both friends and family. The city felt at once familiar and strange at the same time. He realised he had taken some things for granted, like electricity and had forgotten about the power cuts in the country. He laughed aloud when the hot shower he was taking suddenly turned cold and the bathroom plunged into darkness. However, in a short time, it was as if he had never left.

Maryam was constantly asking him questions about England, what it was like, what Auntie's house was like. What about Kulsum? What was she like?

'England is not as nice as you think, Maryam. Life is hard there, especially if you're black as we're classified there.'

One day she asked him about Amina and if he had seen her.

'I saw her only once by chance, believe it or not. She won't forgive me, Maryam, and to be honest, I can't blame her. I did hurt her terribly.'

What Will Be

'Well, she's fine now, Kamal. We correspond occasionally, though she never mentions you, you're dead to her. I got a letter from her a while back; she's married now to a wealthy Englishman.'

Kamal's heart twisted with a pang of jealousy at the news, but he pretended to his sister that he was fine with the news. 'That's good; I'm happy for her.'

Later that night, as he sobbed silently, he couldn't understand himself, couldn't understand why he felt the way he did, he had no reason or right to be jealous. Still, the thought of his Amina with someone else hurt him deeply. He fell into an uneasy sleep and had several strange dreams. In one, he was with Amina, holding and kissing her, then she was suddenly pushing him away while holding a beautiful baby in her arms. He reached his arms for the baby, but the baby laughed at him and held his arms out to another man. Then twin girls were calling him daddy, but when he went to pick them up, they also ran away to another man. He usually never remembered his dreams, but he woke up convinced he had seen all three of his children in his dreams that morning. But who were the men he had dreamed of, was one of them Amina's husband? He believed his children were in heaven, but would they forgive him on The Day Of Judgment? Would they know that he really loved them? That he wished he could have saved them?

With the guilt weighing in heavily on him, Kamal started going off the rails. He would stay out most nights, drinking and partying with his old and new friends to forget about his by now recurring dreams always involving babies. His parents were worried about him, they knew Kulsum had miscarried, but they thought being home would make him feel better. Now he hardly stayed home with them; sometimes, he came home only to shower and change.

As he had no job, after a night of partying, he would come home and sleep all day, get up in the evening, shower, change, eat something and go out again. The new friends he made were mostly gay, some out and openly gay, while others like himself were firmly still in the closet. One of his new friends was a skinny promiscuous Scot with balding ginger hair who was very vain and tried to hide his bald spot with talcum powder. He was new to the city, having arrived in Nairobi to take a position with an international firm and soon developed an obsession with African men. When he couldn't get a normal date, he cruised the streets at night, picked up boys and bringing them back to his flat. His housekeeper, a middle-aged Luo man, was so disgusted with his employer that he left his job even though he had nine children to look after. His wife was not very pleased with him. 'Why do you care what the Mzungu does in his own time? We need the money; we have nine mouths to feed and educate.'

'I'm a good Christian, and I can't in all good conscience work for him. Don't worry, I'll find another position soon.'

The Scot became very friendly with Kamal, and soon they were an item. Everywhere Kamal went, the Scot was there, and although Kamal was faithful, the Scot carried on with his promiscuous life. Kamal's friends warned him. 'Be careful of him. He's been with everyone in the city. He's a man whore,' but he took no notice. They went on safari and other trips together, pretending they were just two friends sharing a room instead of lovers.

Leicester

Back in Leicester, Kulsum, with the help of her parents and friends, began to feel better, slowly getting over the miscarriage and Kamal's betrayal. She went back to her old job and started going out more. She had lost a lot of weight during her depression, so she went out and bought fashionable new clothes. She also cut short her long black hair short and had highlights put in. She went with her friends to cinemas, nightclubs, and cocktail bars, so grateful was she to be out and about. She never went out when Kamal was home because her parents always insisted she stay home with her husband. Since he was away, she had felt as free as a bird, both physically and mentally. She didn't have to wear the traditional salwar kameez anymore. In any case, she had always felt comfortable in her jeans and T-shirts. It was on one of these occasions that her friend Farzana squealed excitedly. 'Oh my God, guess who I just spotted! Afzal!'

Kulsum nearly dropped her mocktail as she turned and saw her old lover for the first time in years.

'Let's call him over,' her friend said, not really needing permission to do so and did it anyway.

Afzal knew the girls through family and community events and went over to say hello. 'Hi girls, how's it going? Can I get you anything?' He had

What Will Be

viewed them collectively, not individually and was shocked when his eyes rested in recognition on Kulsum.

He hadn't expected to see her. She looked the same but somehow different, more beautiful, more assured, a little sadder.

'Hello Afzal,' she smiled at him but inwards, her heart was doing somersaults.

'Hello, Kulsum. Long-time no see, you look great.'

'Thanks, you don't look so bad yourself.'

He spent the evening talking to the group, his eyes and mind firmly on Kulsum. When it was time to go, he offered the girls a lift, but they had their own cars. Since he lived in the direction of Kulsum's house, maybe he could take her? 'Just what I wanted!' he thought, but to Kulsum he said 'No problem, if you want to, I'll take you home.' She agreed, said goodbye to her friends, and the two went off together. They drove in silence to her house, both lost in their own thoughts and emotions.

He stopped just outside her house, turned the ignition off and said, 'Here we are.'

She made no attempt to get out of the car, and he clearly didn't want her to leave.

'I still love you, you know,' he said quietly, 'and I still miss you.'

She was happy to hear him say those words and told him the same.

He pulled her to him and kissed her, and it was as though they had never been apart. He stopped, looked at her with tears in his eyes and said, 'But we can't; you're a married woman.'

The hypocrisy hit Kulsum hard. 'Oh yeah? And you weren't married when we were having an affair, were you? Why was it right then, and wrong now, you bloody hypocrite!'

'I just don't like sharing you.'

'But it was OK for me to share you? Let me out; I can't stand you right now.'

'No, please wait. I was only thinking about you; I don't want your reputation to be ruined. You know people in our community will judge you, but I can get away with it because I am a man.'

What Will Be

She hated hearing this but knew he was right. She also knew through the community grapevine that his wife had left him and was now back in Pakistan. 'What's the deal with your wife then?'

'Well, no one knows the inside story, but I'll tell you. She found out about you and me, don't ask me how, but she demanded a quick divorce and money to set her up in Pakistan, or she would tell everyone you stole her husband. I couldn't let that happen, so I agreed to protect you. Now I'm free and single if you'll have me.'

'I wish I was free and single too, Afzal, but don't worry, I'll ask Kamal for a divorce too when he comes back; he's away in Kenya. I don't love him, and he's certainly never loved me.'

Chapter 26

Nairobi

Kamal's family was getting increasingly worried about his behaviour and his long absences from home. When he was home, he slept all day and hardly ate. He had always been slim, but lately, he looked gaunt and weak. He had never smoked in his life, but now he developed an awful cough that rivalled that of a twenty pack a day smoker. His parents called a family conference, and it was decided that he should go home to his wife. Nairobi was not doing him any good, and they couldn't just stand by and watch him self-destruct anymore.

The very next day, as he was getting ready to go out, his father called him to his room. 'Listen, son, you know we love you and have enjoyed having you home.'

Kamal's heart sank; he knew what was coming; they had found out about him.

'But you know you can't stay here forever. A wife and a family is waiting for you.'

He breathed a sigh of relief; they didn't know, thank God.

'There's a flight to London in two days, and we think you should take it.'

'Two days, Dad, that's too short! Please let me stay a while longer; I really don't want to go back now.'

'You must, you're a husband, not a child, and you have responsibilities to your wife. You're going, and that's the end of the story. You can always come back next year with Kulsum. She's never been to Kenya, and we'd love to see her.'

He couldn't argue with his father and took off to see his boyfriend. He took the stairs to the second floor, rang the doorbell, and the Scot opened the door and enveloped him in a big hug. Kamal broke down immediately, much to the discomfort of the Scot who did not feel comfortable demonstrating his feelings. 'What's the matter?'

'I'm leaving in two days, that's what. I'm going back to the UK.'

'Why man, what's in the dreary old UK? Give me Kenya anytime!'

What Will Be

He hadn't told the Scot he was married, although he suspected that that wouldn't have mattered to him. 'I just have to go, man!'

'But why? You're being as elusive as justice in Kenya,' the Scot laughed at his own joke.

How nice it must be to be white, Kamal thought. You could do and be anything, be gay, be a single mother, a prostitute, be anything without repercussion, without guilt and self-hatred.

'Well, let's not waste any time! We have two whole days together, and you're definitely staying the night!'

The two days went by quickly, and Kamal sadly and reluctantly boarded the flight back to the UK.

Leicester

Kulsum was not looking forward to Kamal's arrival. She had been seeing Afzal and didn't want anything to put a stop to that. Still, it would give her time to broach the subject of divorce, after which she would get married to Afzal, her first love. Her parents were happy he was coming back; they still hoped for at least one grandchild. All of them were shocked when he walked through the door; he looked so ill. He was painfully thin, his skin sallow and sickly. Gone was the healthy man who left them three months ago.

'Kamal, son, are you OK? Why are you so thin? Have you been ill? They haven't told us anything?'

'No, uncle, I have not been ill; I'm fine, just a little tired.' They made a fuss over him as Kulsum pretended she was glad he was home.

He resumed his taxi driving duties and hooked up with guys he'd met when he was with Bale. He had gone to the gym to see Bale, who had made it clear that he wasn't interested anymore; he had a new boyfriend. At night he lay beside an unresponsive Kulsum, sweating profusely and unable to sleep. He had several feverish nights, too and developed sores of the mouth. The family could see he wasn't well and encouraged him to see a doctor. Because Kamal was worried about himself, he agreed to go.

On the appointed day, Kulsum went with him to the doctor at her mother's insistence. The doctor examined him, found he had swellings of the lymph nodes in his armpit, and then decided to send him for a blood test.

What Will Be

A week later, the doctor rang him and asked him to come to his surgery. Again, Kulsum went with him; she felt sorry for him as he looked so awful and skinny. In the doctor's office, they sat side by side and waited to hear what he had to say.

'There's no easy way to say this. I'm very sorry, Mr Khan, but the blood tests show that you contracted HIV some years ago, which has now developed into AIDS. Your immune system is very badly damaged and can no longer fight off serious infections and illnesses. You need to be in hospital immediately, and Mrs Khan, I'm sorry, but you will have to be tested too.'

Kamal started shaking uncontrollably, and Kulsum gasped, horrified. She had always had her suspicions about his sexuality, but this wasn't what she expected to hear. The bastard had put her at risk, too; she might have AIDS herself. She was furious, the realisation dawning on her that her twins, had they survived, might have had H.I.V. Composing herself with great difficulty, she asked, 'Can I do the test now, please, doctor?'

'I don't see why not. I'll treat it as an emergency.'

He called in his nurse and asked her to do the test as a matter of urgency. Kamal couldn't look at Kulsum, so ashamed was he. He prayed that he hadn't infected her; his mind turned back to all those years in Kenya when he had his dalliances with his friend and the Scot and others since. He couldn't be sure who had infected him and given him this death sentence.

A few minutes later, the nurse came in with the results and handed them to the doctor. Terrified, Kulsum held her breath; if the bastard had infected her, she was going to kill him, sin, or no sin.

'I'm pleased to say you're in the clear, Mrs Khan.'

She gave a silent thank you to God, stood up and, with tears of relief streaming down her cheeks, walked out of the surgery.

Kamal followed her silently, miserably. When they got to the house, she told him she wanted a divorce immediately; everyone would understand that she couldn't stay married to a gay man with AIDS, and from now on, he was dead to her. He begged her not to tell her parents, but that was the first thing she did; it was too big a secret to keep to herself.

They listened to her in shock and disbelief; her mother at first refused to believe her.

'You're lying; you've always had it in for him, ever since you were married!'

She convinced her mother she wasn't lying and showed them her negative result certificate. Kulsum's father, beside himself with anger, called Kamal and demanded that he divorce his daughter immediately and get out of their house. He was forced to say Talak three times, and she was divorced just like that. Divorce wasn't taken lightly in Islam, but in this case, it was a must. 'Do not darken our door again. Your poor parents, they will die of shame when we tell them about this.'

With those awful words ringing in his ears, he quickly put his belongings in a suitcase and left the house, not knowing where he was going. He was to end up sleeping on various sofas and in various beds with random strangers as his condition worsened.

Southampton

While inspecting her rose garden, Amina heard the house phone ringing and instantly being answered. Her nanny then called out to her that she was wanted on the phone.

'Hello,' she answered cheerfully.

'Hello Amina, it's me, Maryam, your old friend from Nairobi.' She hadn't heard from her for years, so she was wondering what the call was about. After the pleasantries, Maryam said, 'Sorry to bother you, Amina, but Kamal wants to see you.'

'Why does he want to see me? We have nothing to say to each other.'

'Please Amina, he is dying, he's in hospital and has only a more few days'

'Oh, I'm sorry, Maryam, what happened? What's wrong with him?'

'He has AIDS.'

'Oh my God, poor thing! How did he get it from his wife?'

'No, he didn't get it from her. She tested negative.'

'Then how?'

'Amina, because you're a friend, I'll tell you what I know. Apparently, he had gay lovers, and they think a Scottish man infected him. Kamal told me that the Scot has already died.'

What Will Be

Amina was stunned into silence. She had never ever, even in her wildest dreams, thought Kamal could be gay. She was suddenly relieved that he'd left her, she had had a very lucky escape, and knew that God was looking after her. She knew she didn't have H.I.V. because she had had all sorts of blood tests when she was pregnant with her daughter. 'How long has he got?'

'Not long, and I would be really happy if you went to visit him, it'll be good for him to see someone from home. He has no one there, and the Pakistani community has shunned and rejected him; our parents have disowned him too once the news arrived in Nairobi. His wife got married two days after he was admitted to hospital, can you imagine that? Callous cow!'

Amina found it incredibly hard to believe that the Kamal she knew, strong and handsome, was the same one being described by his sister. 'I'm so sorry, Maryam, of course, I'll go; give me the name of the hospital.'

Amina was so happy with her life; she couldn't be angry at Kamal anymore. If anything, he had done her a favour. If he hadn't left her for his cousin, she wouldn't have met Dylan, and even worse, it would have been her now going through the ignominy of having a gay husband dying of AIDS. Her life was sorted; she had a thriving company that was growing by the day, bringing in money that she didn't really need; Dylan's business had expanded and diversified even more. He was now one of the richest land and property owners in the country. She had a lovely mansion in the best area in the city. Ayan had finally married Omar, who was now a partner in a prestigious law firm, and was working and living happily in London. Anab was thriving in old age and Amina herself was now pregnant with her second child. She felt that she could afford a little generosity and sympathy towards Kamal, who had hurt her so badly all those years ago. She had never told Dylan the full story, although she had told him about her ex, Kamal. Much as she loved him, there were certain things she could never share with him, he would be too shocked, especially if he ever found out that his wife was complicit in a murder. That night when he came home, she told him about Maryam's phone call and said she was obliged to go as she'd promised her old friend that she would.

'Do you want me to come with you, darling?'

What Will Be

That's why she loved him, he never questioned her over what she wanted to do, and he was always just supportive. How like him to worry about her and not the prospect of her seeing her ex again, even though he was dying.

'No thanks, darling. I'll be fine. He hasn't got long, so I'll leave tomorrow. I'll take the first train and be home in the evening.'

Leicester

She had three and a half hours on the train to think about poor Kamal and what a tragic turn his life had taken. She kept thinking back to Nairobi and tried to remember any signs he gave off about his sexuality. She had been too young, she realised and wouldn't even have known if he was gay because, at the time, she didn't even know that gay people existed; she had been in her own innocent bubble, wrapped up in Kamal.

When she arrived at Leicester London Road station, she took a taxi to Leicester General Hospital. She made her way to the intensive care unit. She asked the nurse on duty which bed he was in, and the nurse told her he wasn't allowed visitors as he was in a critical condition.

'Sister, please, I have come a long way to see him, and he has specifically asked for me. I am an old family friend.'

'Make it quick then, I hear his ex-wife has refused to see him to even say goodbye, poor man.'

Amina went to his bed and drew the curtain back. The shock of what she saw brought tears to her eyes. He was hooked up with drips, he had sores around his mouth, and his lovely thick, dark hair was no more. In its place were thin wispy strands; he looked like a wizened old man. 'Kamal,' she called softly.

He opened his eyes and said weakly, 'Amina, you came.'

'Of course, I came Kamal; how could I not. How are you? I am so sorry about what happened to you.'

'I wasn't sure you'd come, I told Maryam you wouldn't want to see me, but she insisted on telling you. I told her I just wanted to see you once more before I die.'

He noticed her swelling stomach. 'You're going to be a mother.'

'Yes,' she said, knowing both were thinking about the child he made her abort.

What Will Be

'I'm sorry, Amina, for everything. I always wanted children; you know. I'm sorry I made you get rid of ours; not a day goes by when I don't think about it. You know, I have a recurring dream about a little boy. He's always smiling, looking up at me and calling me dad, but he's also always running away from me. There are also other people in my dreams, people I don't know. Will you ever forgive me?'

At the mention of the little boy, Amina's heart twisted with anger and sadness; maybe he was dreaming about her little boy who she got rid of. She hated him at that moment, but the words slipped out. 'I forgive you.'

With fresh tears in his eyes, he thanked her. 'Are you happy?'

'Yes, I'm very happy, I have a husband who I love and who loves me, a beautiful daughter, and now we're waiting for this little miracle,' she said, patting her stomach.

'And here I am with no one and dying alone. I asked for only two people to ask for their forgiveness, you and my ex-wife, my cousin. She refused to come but sent me a message saying I should go to hell where I will surely be going and that she'll never forgive me. I don't blame her but look at the difference between you two. You are a good person Amina, and I am so sorry for all the pain I caused you. Believe me, I have paid for that.'

'It doesn't matter now, Kamal'

'Yes, it does; look at me now, lying in hospital, dying of a shameful disease, disowned by my family, all alone. I go to my Lord as I came into this world, naked and alone. Pray for me, Amina, even though I don't deserve any prayers.'

She looked at him sadly and stood up. 'I will pray for you, but now I've got to get going. I need to catch the next train back home.'

'Please don't go yet; stay a while. I don't want to die alone,' he begged with tears in his eyes.

So, she sat by his bedside doing the one thing she never thought she'd do as she held his hand. 'You won't die. There's new medication now.'

'Too late for me,' he rasped painfully. He started coughing heavily, a sight painful to see as his skeletal chest barely rose.

She got him a glass of water, from which he took one sip before the coughing started again. 'I'll get the nurse,' she pressed the call button above his bed, but he clung tightly to her hand and wouldn't let go.

What Will Be

He gave one last gasp of breath as his life slipped away. Just like that, Kamal was gone.

The nurse arrived to find Amina still holding his hand. She took one look at him and knew he was gone. 'Come on, love,' she said gently. 'Say goodbye now.'

'What happens to him now?' she asked. 'Well, as he has no family, the hospital will make the funeral arrangements and bury him.'

'Please bury him in a Muslim cemetery; he was Muslim, you know.'

'We can't make special arrangements for him, he's unclaimed, and so the state will take care of his cremation or burial.'

'Please then, could you make sure he's buried and not cremated?'

'I can certainly ask. Would you like to come to the funeral, so he has at least one person who knew him in this life?'

'No, I won't be coming, and I have to get going now, or I'll miss my train home. Goodbye, Sister.'

'Oh, wait, is your name, is it Amina? If so, he asked me to give you something,'

'Yes, I'm Amina,' she replied as the nurse went to her drawer and withdrew an envelope with her name on it. Amina took it, walked out of the hospital, grabbed the first taxi she saw, and was soon on the train, speeding back home to her husband.

On the train, she opened the envelope and saw Kamal's familiar writing. 'My darling Amina, I just wanted you to know that despite everything, I have always loved you. Even as my life spiralled out of control, I always thought of you and what my life might have been like if only I had the guts to say no to my parents and refuse to marry my cousin. Would I ever have gone for a man? Would I be lying here dying of a shameful disease? I don't know. I hope you find it in your heart to forgive me and think of me with kindness. I remember us talking about Somali poetry on several occasions and how much you loved it. With great difficulty I have managed to find Raage Ugaas's poem which you used to love. I find it sad that it was me and not you who was made to accept another. Read it and think of me. Please forgive me and pray for me to find peace in the afterlife.'

What Will Be

Amina started reading the poem by one of the greatest Somali poets with a lump in her throat. A tear traced its way down her cheek when she finished reading it.

A Broken Betrothal

Night had fallen, the doors were shut and all men were asleep
Thunder resounded and the rain was echoing like a thousand rifle-shots
But still my shouts of lamentation could be heard-
People took them for the roar of an approaching lion.
Sore are my ribs; sore are the very bones of my spine-
Bones which are to men as a support-pole is to a hut-
And dammed up and unseeing are my eyes.
Only God knows fully the hurt that makes me wail like this!
A hawk cannot fly with an injured wing-
A broken-backed horse will not try to rise and run-
Many and loud are the growls of camels
When they are stricken by thirst.
A man whose eyes and rib-cage are not sound
Cannot avenge the wrongs that he has suffered,
And a man whose heart is afflicted with disease
Will not be making merry at a wedding- feast.
I grieve over my sorrow like a young girl
Whose mother has gone to rest in the other world?
And whose father has brought home another wife
And made the girl sleep at the entrance of the new wife's hut.
I am a man whose betrothed was made to accept another-
I am a man who had seen a spring full of water
But whose thirst must stay unquenched forever.
THE END.

References:

Somalia A crisis of Famine and War, Edward R. Ricciuti

An Anthology of Somali Poetry, Translated by B.W. Andrzejewski with Sheila Andrezejewski

What Will Be